Stanley Smartpants and the Harbour Mystery

Extracts from Children's Reviews

"... a mind boggling
throughout, I loved
the best I've
Georgia

"It was stunning,
I couldn't put the book down ... really
entertaining .... hilariously funny ... I would
recommend this book to everyone I know."
Max New Panayi, age 10

"I love this book .... hilariously funny ...
I can't wait for the next book."
Luca Brais, age 8

"... a detective story like no other
.... funny, also very exciting."
Daisy Platt, age 11

"This book is brilliant, once you start reading it
you never want to put it down .... It is different
from any other book in a fantastic way. I love it!
.... it is purr-fect for my age group. 5 stars
Evelyn Barter, age 9

"I liked the book because it had a lot of mystery
.... the book overall was 5 stars and I would
recommend it to 8+
Hayden Eccles, age 9

Praise for the first novel in this series,

Stanley Smartpants and the Mackerel Robberies

Just a few of the comments received in e-mails from children

To Mick

ALEXANDER MARTIN

with best wishes

Martin

Stanley Smartpants and the Harbour Mystery

Illustrations by Rebecca Clements
www.stanleysmartpants.co.uk

First Published in Great Britain in 2012 by
Ambassador Publishing Co.
38 Harris Crescent
Needingworth
Cambridgeshire
PE27 4TE

A CIP Catalogue of this book is available from
the British Library

ISBN 978-0-9560758-1-9

Illustrated by Rebecca Clements

Designed and typeset by
Chandler Book Design

Printed and bound in
Great Britain by
Ashford Colour Press

FOR JACK AND KATIE

Author's Note

The fictional towns of Cat-Haven-on-Sea and
Brixcat are based respectively on Paignton and
Brixham in South Devon

Acknowledgements

I would like to extend my thanks to the following people who in one way or another have made a positive contribution to the Stanley Smartpants novels, and most especially to all the children, who are too numerous to mention, who have provided me with invaluable feedback.

My warmest thanks to the ever talented Becky Clements for all her marvellous illustrations which have helped enormously to bring my characters to life. My thanks also to John Chandler who has designed the book cover and prepared the manuscript for printing. My special thanks also to the nine children who kindly read and commented on the manuscript, and whose names appear on the first two pages.

I am particularly keen to encourage children to take part in the creative process of writing a novel. There are three instances in the book where I have used children's contributions, and these follow with the names of the children concerned.

STANLEY'S OUTFITS

Front Cover and Chapter 2: We all just love the front cover design, which was created by **Francesca Suckling, age 9, of Fen Drayton Primary School in Cambridgeshire.**

Stanley's other outfits, described in the following chapters, were designed by:

Chapter 14: Hannah Donaldson, age 9,
Market Deeping Primary School

Chapter 19: Charlie Stewart, age 9,
Market Deeping Primary School

Chapter 31: Morgan Whybrow, age 11,
Fen Drayton Primary School

Chapter 37: Chloe Jones, age 9,
Market Deeping Primary School

Chapter 44: Katy Langdon, age 9,
Oldway Primary School

Chapter 47: Amy Blackledge, age 10,
Heritage Park Primary School

JOKES TOLD BY JUMPING JACK

Chapter 8: Twelve red cats – **Heidi Surfleet**

Chapter 9: Banana – **Claudia Waller**

Chapter 13: Hat and scarf – **Chloe Cotterell**

Chapter 19: Cat and Comma – **Andrew Michael**

CAT IDEAS

We invited children to make up names of businesses, places, expressions etc that had some cat reference. Here are the ones Alexander Martin has used:

Cast of Characters

(breed if known)

A. CAT-POLICE CATS   In order of appearance

Detective Sergeant Stanley Smartpants
(Blue Tabby Point Birman)

Our hero and principal detective of the Cat-Haven-on-Sea Cat-Police. Intelligent, handsome and beautifully dressed, he has a fine collection of cool trousers. He writes and recites poems about events that occur in the story, and is loved by all the female cats. Has his own website.

Detective Chief Inspector Derek Dimwit
(moggie)

A plain black and white moggie. The not very bright boss of the Cat-Haven Cat-Police, he is slow on the uptake and easily offended. Stammers when he's flustered, and frequently makes a fool of himself in front of his staff.

Cat-Constable Marmalade Marmaduke
(Red Tabby Shorthair)

Similar in colour to a jar of Seville Orange marmalade. Always eating toast and marmalade. A bit accident prone. Has a great sense of humour.

Cat-Constable Tammy Tickletummy
(Seal Point Siamese)

A real fussy diva, particularly when it comes to food. Fully aware of her cat-rights in the work place, she stands up for herself and complains about anything that upsets her. Likes her tummy tickled, particularly when she is upset.

Cat-Constable Jumping Jack *(American Wirehair)*

Young, frisky and enthusiastic, he's always jumping around. His frizzy hair stands up on end as if he's had an electric shock. Loves to tell jokes. Has lots of admirers amongst the female cats. Marmaduke's best friend.

Cat-Constable Playful Pamela
(Black Smoke & White Cornish Rex)

Enjoys playing games. She has long, graceful legs and loves to dance to Tammy's iPod Shuffle. Tammy's best friend.

Cadet-Cat Soppy Cynthia
(Red Spotted Tabby Munchkin)

Has short legs and a short tail and looks a bit like a squirrel. Is helpless and makes stupid mistakes. She adores Jack and likes to try and tickle herself so she can carry on laughing at his jokes.

Cat-Sergeant Cheerful Charlie

The desk sergeant at the Cat-Haven Cat-Police station.

Cadet-Cat Studious Stephen
(Blue Cream & White Devon Rex)

Wears wire-framed nose glasses and is always reading books that other cats are not interested in. He likes to think himself superior to the other cats, and loves to show off his knowledge. Actually he's a pain in the bum!

Cadet-Cat Vacant Vincent
(Manx)

Frequently stares into space. Suffers from Manx Syndrome, an unfortunate bowel disorder that afflicts some Manx cats. Constantly has to ask in meetings if he can "go for a poo".

Apple Pie Annie
(California Spangled)

American forensic scientist-cat on loan from Catmel-on-Sea Cat-Police in California, USA. Usually wears huge blue glasses. Loves her apple pie.

Greta the Grumbler
(Red Classic Tabby Maine Coon)

The cat-police station cook and the cat-police secretary, known as the Chief Assistant to the Assistant Chief. Is always grumbling and feels that she is not appreciated.

Cadet-Cat Skatie Katie
(American Wirehair)

Jumping Jack's sister. A former Cat-Olympic ice-skating champion, and skating coach at the skating rink. Has just joined the Cat-Haven Cat-Police.

B. OTHER CATS   In order of appearance

Nosey Nathan

Security-cat at Brixcat Harbour. Has a humungous nose that looks like a squashed banana, and produces an unfortunate amount of yellowy green snot.

Bouncing Bert
(Norwegian Forest Cat)

Assistant Harbour Master-cat. Bounces along on his paws when he's running, as if bouncing on a trampoline. ***A Suspect.***

Bosun Brian

Harbour Master-cat at Brixcat Harbour. ***A Victim***

Ship-Shape Shane
(Norwegian Forest)

Commodore-cat at the Brixcat Yacht Club. A humungous black cat with a scruffy black and grey beard. *A suspect.*

Little Big Ben
(Bombay)

A clock maker and school friend of Jack's. His grandfather started the family business, with a contract to carry out maintenance on Big Ben at the Cat-Parliament.

Precious Gemma
(Turkish Angora)

Sales assistant at Cat Diamonds "R" Us. Bosun Brian's wife. *A suspect.*

Fishercat Freddie
(American Black Bombay)

Fishes for mackerel from Brixcat Harbour. *A Suspect.*

Sir Lancelot Smiles-a-Lot
(Burmese)

A squintillionaire politician-cat with gleaming white teeth, member of the Cat-Parliament at Catminster, and owner of a humungous yacht moored in Brixcat Harbour. *A Victim and A Suspect.*

Pretty Peaches
(Australian Mist)
Sales assistant at Cat Diamonds 'R' Us. A gorgeous peach coloured cat and special friend of Stanley.

Chop Suey Charlie
Owner of the Chop Suey-Cat Chinese Restaurant.

Hing Hong Big Pong
Part-time waiter-cat at the Chop Suey-Cat restaurant. Works on farm cleaning house of pigs and chickens.

Hong Po Fried Rice
Dice playing customer in Chop Suey-Cat restaurant.

Sweet and Sour Wing Wang
Dice playing customer in Chop Suey-Cat restaurant.

Yong Kong Kevin
Waiter-cat in Chop Suey-Cat restaurant.

Willy Splish
(Maine Coon)
Owner of Splash Splosh Painters and Decorators. ***A Suspect.***

Corky
A snow white, blue-eyed, and very ~~naughty~~ fun-loving kitten.

Simile Emily

Receptionist-cat at the Cat-Haven Chronicle. Loves using similes when speaking.

Poisonous Paddy the Pen
(American Burmese)
Editor-cat at the Cat-Haven Chronicle.

Eberneezer the Sneezer

Has a medical problem which causes him to sneeze frequently.

Vodka Valentina
(Russian Blue)
Waitress-cat at the Bling Bling Bar and sister of Yuri Katakov. A special friend of Marmalade Marmaduke.

Yuri Katakov
(Russian Blue)
Russian ice-skating champion and part-time dishwasher-cat. Good friends with Marmaduke. Had been a suspect in the Mackerel Robberies case.

Colourful Christine

A blind cat. Stanley's next door neighbour.

Steve

An incredibly talented German Shepherd. Christine's Guide Dog. Speaks cat-lingo.

Wanda

Waitress-cat at the Sea View Café.

Snugsy & Bugsy
(Maine Coons)

The ~~naughty~~ fun-loving kitten twins of Greta the Grumbler.

Dodgy Dave
(Havana Brown)

Solicitor-cat, representing Willy Splish. Has a strong cockney accent.

Mackerel Mike
(Maine Coon)

Fishes for mackerel from Brixcat Harbour. ***A Suspect.***

Groovy Grace

Receptionist-cat at the Cat-Haven Arsenal.

Firearms Fergie

Boss of the Cat-Haven Arsenal.

Muliplication Megan

Book-keeper-cat at the Cat-Haven Arsenal.

Wednesday 7ᵗʰ December

Stanley stood in the doorway gazing at his boss, shaking his head in disbelief. It was shortly after half past nine in the morning, and Chief Inspector Derek Dimwit of the Cat-Haven Cat-Police was fast asleep. His screechy, scratchy, squeaky snoring caused Stanley to wonder if he might be ill. But it had a curious and repetitive sing-song rhythm, and sounded like an express train clattering through a railway station at top speed.

Stanley coughed, but there was no response. He coughed again, but this time louder. "Ahem! Ahem!"

At last Derek opened one eye and looked at Stanley suspiciously.

"There's been a robbery on a yacht moored in Brixcat Harbour, Chief," said Stanley.

"It doesn't sound very important. Tell me about it later, Stan." Derek closed his unblinking eye and snuggled deeper into the comfort of his padded leather chair.

"We can't let the grass grow under our paws on this one, Chief. The yacht belongs to the squintillionaire politician-cat, Sir Lancelot Smiles-a-Lot."

"I hear what you say, Stan, but you should never wake a cat when he's in the middle of a cat-nap," said Derek sleepily, his eyes still tight shut.

Detective Sergeant Stanley Smartpants was not to be put off so easily. "Your cousin, the Mayor, won't be pleased if we don't deal with this quickly."

Before Stanley could say any more, a cat who was similar in colour to a jar of Seville orange marmalade rushed into Derek's office, two slices of toast and marmalade clutched in his paws. "It's an emergency, Chief," he spluttered. "Tammy's fallen into the chocolate pudding!"

At the mention of chocolate pudding Derek Dimwit was instantly awake and alert. "What chocolate pudding?" he said, licking his whiskers in anticipation.

"Chocolate pudding!" exclaimed Stanley. "That is sooooo cool!" His face broke into a beaming smile, and he waggled his chocolate brown ears.

Cat-Constable Marmalade Marmaduke, a Red Tabby Shorthair, took a bite out of both slices of toast and marmalade at virtually the same time. Oodles and oodles of crumbs from his mouth fell onto the carpet.

Derek was annoyed. "You shouldn't stroll into my office eating toast, Marmaduke. You should show me more respect. And you should have knocked."

Marmaduke shrugged his shoulders. With his mouth still full of toast he said, "I couldn't, Chief. My paws were unavailable." Pointedly he looked at his paws, still clutching his toast. "Anyway they were sticky."

"F-f-f-f-f-forget it, Marmaduke," stammered Derek. "What's this about a chocolate pudding? Why didn't one of you cats come and wake me? You know how much I love chocolate pudding!"

"Me too, Chief," said Marmaduke. "I'm reeally, reeeally, reeeeally hungry!"

"Let's go and sort this out," said Stanley. He hitched up his colourful trousers and strode out of Derek's office.

As he opened the door of the Crime Room, Stanley was greeted by an incredible scene. Cat-Constable Tammy Tickletummy, a gorgeous Seal Point Siamese, who was normally easy to recognise on account of her soft white coat, was standing on top of the conference table, dripping chocolate, and looking as miserable as a wet weekend in winter. She was covered from whisker to paw in Catbury's Dairy Milk cat-chocolate pudding, and no cat could have guessed the colour of her fur.

Cat-Constable Jumping Jack was winding himself up to jump onto the table. He had announced that he was going to lick Tammy to pieces, and was being egged on by the female cadet-cats. Just as Jack leapt onto the table, Derek came marching into the room. And the moment he saw the chaotic scene in front of him his plain, black and white face turned purple. "What are you cats doing?" he demanded.

But no-one was listening.

"Why don't we have a chocolate dance," said Marmaduke. "Pamela, switch on Tammy's iPod Shuffle. Let's have some music."

"Now look here c-c-c-c-cats," said Derek. "This is unacceptable b-b-b-b-behaviour." Derek had an unfortunate habit of stammering when he was flustered.

"It's our chocolate break, Chief," said Jack, tongue in cheek. "Tammy will tell you, we can do what we like during our breaks."

Tammy was usually quick to point out their cat-rights in the work place, but she still looked miserable and said nothing.

Jack jumped up onto the table and pretended to trip over his own feet. He was an American Wirehair, a breed of cat that has frizzy fur. In Jack's case it was so spiky it looked as if he had had an electric shock! He fell into Tammy's arms. "Oops!" he said, "sorry Tammy." He didn't look very sorry, and took the opportunity to open his mouth as wide as possible. His tongue darted in and out with the speed of Jerry trying to escape from Tom, and with each dart of his tongue he licked as much chocolate as he could from Tammy's fur.

The situation was getting out of hand, and Stanley took charge. Conveniently he had a spoon in his trouser pocket, a spoon that was soon to be put to serious chocolate use! He banged it several times on the edge of a desk.

Every cat in the Crime Room knew that Stanley was about to deliver one of his famous poems, and they all fell silent.

> *"A choc'late pudding is for cats a treat,*
> *And into it to fall is not so neat.*
> *Why Tammy fell into the pud we cannot guess,*
> *A shower is what she needs, a lick would*
> *make a mess.*
> *Nor do we know why Jack would like to lick*
> *her clean.*
> *'Cos Jack, my friend, you do not know where else*
> *she's been!"*

There was a lot of noisy laughter and clapping from those cats who were in the room. Stanley's poems always went down well.

Tammy was a bit put out. "You shouldn't be making a joke at my expense, Sergeant. It's against my cat-rights in the work place. And it's not fair!"

"Come on Tammy," said Marmaduke, "lighten up."

Tammy glowered at Marmaduke. "I thought you would have taken my side, Marmy."

"I *am* taking your side, Tammy. It's not so serious, now is it?"

Before Tammy could reply Playful Pamela jumped in. "Come on, Tammy, I'll take you to the showers. The Sarge is right, you need to get cleaned up."

Stanley looked round for Soppy Cynthia, but couldn't see her anywhere. It was she who had taken the telephone call reporting the robbery. "Where's Cynthia gone?"

"I'm here, Sarge," she said from the far corner of the Crime Room. Cadet-Cat Soppy Cynthia was an unusual breed of cat, a Red Spotted Tabby Munchkin, with short legs and a short tail. And she looked unusual too. When she sat up on her haunches with her paws off the ground, as she did now, she looked more like a squirrel than a cat!

"Cynthia, just refresh my memory about the telephone call you took."

"What telephone call?" said Cynthia. She had a puzzled look on her face.

Stanley sighed inwardly. "You said the Harbour Master-cat from Brixcat Harbour called."

"Oh, yes," said Cynthia, blushing heavily. "Silly me! I was so interested in the chocolate pudding that I almost forgot about it."

"So, what did the Harbour Master-cat say?" asked Stanley.

"He said that Sir Lancelot Smiles-a-Lot has

suffered a serious robbery. The safe on his boat has been broken into, and loads of jewellery and cash has been stolen."

"Is that all?"

"Isn't that enough, Sarge," interrupted Jack, winking at Marmaduke, "having cash and jewellery stolen?"

Stanley turned towards Jack, and raised a disapproving eyebrow. "Did he say anything else, Cynthia?"

"He also said he knows who stole it all," said Cynthia.

"Who was it?" asked Stanley.

"He didn't say."

"Didn't you ask him, Cynthia?"

"No," said Cynthia, her face reddening. "I was so excited that I forgot to ask him."

"Shall I ring him back and find out, Sarge?" asked Jack.

Derek butted in without thinking. "No, don't worry Jack, Stanley and I are on our way there now. After we've had some chocolate pudding, of course! We'll ask him ourselves. It's good to know that the crime is already solved. I wonder who did it?"

The Same Day

Birman cats are perhaps the most beautiful cats in the world. Stanley Smartpants certainly thought so. Stanley was a Birman with striking, sapphire blue eyes. He had a soft coat of creamy-white fur and a fluffy, bushy tail. He had lovely brown markings on his handsome face and gorgeous chocolate brown ears. He was well known in the Cat-Haven Cat-Police as a cat who was always smartly dressed, and his wardrobe was chock-a-block with squintillions of fantastic, stylish trousers! Today he was wearing a pair of snazzy yellow trousers with occasional clusters of small green and red diamonds, a turquoise blue waistcoat with red buttons, and a bow tie with red, green and yellow diamonds.

In complete contrast Derek Dimwit was dressed in shabby black trousers and a dirty green fleece over a threadbare grey shirt. Derek was not a pedigree cat. He was, quite simply, an ordinary black and white moggie!

* * * *

Stanley and Derek drove into Cat-Haven-on-Sea town centre, through the level crossing and on down towards the sea. They turned right at the Cat Odeon and passed the new Crazy Golf. It was now called Crazy Adventure Golf for Crazy Cats, and had lots of pirates and water and rocks and stuff. They drove on out of Cat-Haven along the shore road. When they reached the outskirts of Brixcat they went down the steep hill that led to the town. They pulled into the Harbour entrance. A self important cat in a Securicat uniform bustled out of the glass booth and held up his paw. He was seriously overweight and had a paunchy stomach that hung over the belt of his trousers. But his nose! That was unbelievable! It was humungously long, and as black, as bruised, as squishy squashy, and as unappealing as an over ripe banana.

"Can't you see that we're the cat-police?" said Derek rudely. "Where can we find the Harbour Master-cat?"

"I need to see your identification," said the security-cat, puffing out his paunch.

"I'm Detective Sergeant Smartpants, and this is my colleague, Chief Inspector Dimwit." Stanley flipped open his wallet, and showed his warrant card. "Where can we find the Harbour Master-cat?"

"What's your name?" asked Derek, even more rudely.

The security-cat hesitated. "They … er …. call me Nosey Nathan," he said, his cheeks reddening.

Derek couldn't help himself. He laughed out loud.

"It's not what you think," said Nathan, his cheeks getting even redder. "It's got nothing to do with my nose. It's because it's my job to know what's going on." Rather foolishly he tapped the side of his nose.

"You could have fooled me," said Derek, and laughed some more. "Perhaps it's because you're always poking your nose into other people's business?"

Stanley nudged Derek in the ribs. "I think I just need to know where the Harbour Master-cat's office is."

"Up those stairs," said Nathan, pointing to a wide, stone staircase. "His office is on the right. You can't miss it." He turned away and went back into his booth.

It was a one storey building at first floor level. The first door that they saw at the top of the staircase had a sign announcing **Harbour Master-cat**. The door was closed. Stanley knocked lightly and waited. There was no reply from inside. He opened the door wide, and stood in the doorway. The office was empty.

"Hmm," said Stanley. "No-one here."

"Shall we wait?" said Derek.

They waited for five minutes, then went back down the stairs and approached the security-cat once more.

"He doesn't seem to be there," said Stanley. "Would you please buzz the other offices and see if you can find him."

Nosey Nathan picked up the phone. It was an old fashioned telephone with a long flex. He seemed flustered and caught his nose in the flex. Derek laughed. After speaking to several other cats Nathan shook his head. "He's not in any of the offices up there. Strange. I definitely didn't see him come down. I'll try his mobile."

There was no reply.

"This is really odd," said Derek, turning to Stanley. "You would have thought he'd wait for us after calling us, wouldn't you?"

Suddenly there was a loud shout and a cat came running towards them along the quay. He wasn't so much running as bouncing along on his paws, as if the quay was a long and narrow trampoline. He was an overweight black Norwegian Forest cat.

"That's Bouncing Bert," said Nathan. "He's the assistant Harbour Master-cat. Everyone calls him Bouncy."

Bouncing Bert was sweating and his face was flushed. He was breathing heavily. "Nosey, there's been an accident. Get the cat-police down here fast."

"Excuse me, sir," said Stanley, "we *are* the cat-police." He flipped open his wallet. "I'm Detective Sergeant Smartpants. What's happened?"

"It's the Harbour Master-cat. He's had an accident."

"Where is he?"

"Follow me, Sergeant."

* * * *

Stanley and Derek followed Bouncing Bert to a large brick building, which was situated at the far end of the harbour. It was the fish warehouse, where the fishercats offloaded the fish they had caught at sea, and prepared them for the Fish Market in Cat-Haven. As the three cats entered the building, a large ginger cat pushed past them, carrying a huge tray of mackerel on his head. Stanley and Derek breathed in the wonderful smells of sea, salt and freshly caught fish. Their noses tingled and they licked their lips.

Just inside the building there was a small office on the right hand side.

"In there," was all Bouncing Bert said.

Stanley opened the door and went in. A large, smoky-grey cat, with a weather-beaten face, lay flat on his back in the middle of the room. His clothes were soaking wet, and his eyes were shut. He remained completely still. Not a whisker as much as trembled. Stanley walked slowly towards him. On close inspection he could clearly see blood on the cat's forehead, and a huge bruise behind his left ear.

"He's stone dead," said Stanley over his shoulder to Derek.

"He c-c-c-c-can't be dead," said Derek. "He rang the cat-police station only an hour ago!"

"Maybe so, but he's dead now."

"Goodness g-g-g-g-gracious."

"Me and a couple of other cats have just pulled

him out of the sea," said Bouncing Bert, who had followed them into the office. "We thought he'd fallen in, and struck his head on something. We weren't sure if he was dead or not."

"Did you see what happened?"

"No, I was just walking along the quay when I saw something out of the corner of my eye. I looked down into the water, and that's when I saw him. He'd obviously tripped on something. I went to get a rope to throw down to him, but when I lowered it into the water he didn't try to grab hold of it."

"Just a minute," interrupted Stanley. "Are you saying that he was already dead, or that he wasn't dead at that point?"

"I'm not sure," said Bert hesitantly.

"Go on," said Stanley

"I got two of the fishercats to help me. They dived in and hauled him onto one of the boats. From there we got him into the office here. Then I went for help. And that's when I bumped into you two."

"Was he dead when you got him into the office here?" asked Derek.

"Yes, he was."

"I see," said Stanley. "Where are the two cats who helped you pull him out? And why didn't at least one of them stay with him when you went for help?"

"I don't know where they are. And I've no idea why one of them didn't stay with him."

"Who *are* these two cats?"

"They're both fishercats. Fishercat Freddie and Mackerel Mike. Look, I must call the Harbour Master-cat's wife, Sergeant. Can you excuse me?"

"Go ahead, but I'll want to talk to you again, so please don't go anywhere. And if you bump into these other two cats, tell them I want to see them. I'll either be here or in the Harbour Master-cat's office."

"No worries," said Bouncing Bert, and off he bounced. "I'll be in my office when you need me. It's next to the Harbour Master-cat's office."

"Good idea, Stan."

Stanley looked puzzled. He didn't know what Derek was talking about. "What is, Chief?" he queried.

"Taking over the Harbour Master-cat's office. We'll need to have a base here for the time being. And let's be honest," said Derek, grinning from ear to ear, "he won't be needing it now, will he?"

"Hmm," said Stanley. "Do you remember Fishercat Freddie, Chief?"

"Can't say I do," replied Derek.

"You must remember, Chief. It was our last big case, the Mackerel Robberies. He was the brother of Harriet Fishnet, you know the cat who got hit on the head on Torcat Beach. And when she woke up she discovered that some of her mackerel catch was missing."

Derek's eyes widened and you could almost hear his brain clanking away as he struggled to remember.

"Oh, yes," he said finally. "I do remember now. But so what?"

"Just making an observation, Chief."

"Anyway, Stan, do you think the Harbour Master-cat's death has got anything to do with the robbery on that politician-cat's boat?"

"Good question, Chief! Maybe, maybe not. And I'm not so sure it was an accident. Look at that bruise behind his ear."

Derek bent down and rested his paw on the dead cat's back. "Yes," he said. "It's as clear as the fact that a three-legged mouse can't run very fast. He was obviously hit on the head with something. It's obvious. He was murdered!"

The Same Day

"Let's go and have another word with the security-cat, Chief," said Stanley.

"I'll call the office first, and tell Jack and Marmaduke to get down here fast." Derek pulled his mobile out of his pocket and called the station.

After only two rings a deep voice answered. "Hello, Cat-Haven Cat-Police, Cheerful Charlie speaking. How can I help you?"

While Derek spoke to Cheerful Charlie, Stanley went back to the glass booth. Nosey Nathan came out of the booth and looked uncertainly at Stanley.

Stanley checked his watch. It was ten minutes past twelve. "Have you been on duty all morning?" he asked.

"Yes," said the security-cat hesitantly. "I started at eight."

"How many cats have climbed those stairs in the last hour?"

"That's a bit difficult to say. There are comings

and goings all the time. There are seven offices up there, you know."

"Don't you at least keep a record of visitors?"

"No."

"Not very good security," said Stanley. "Are these stairs the only way of getting to the first floor?"

"Yes."

"How many visitor-cats, cats that are unknown to you, have been up there this morning?"

"About four," said the security-cat, but he didn't sound very positive.

Derek approached. "I've told the office that the Harbour Master-cat is dead, Stan," he said.

Stanley was pleased that Derek hadn't blurted out that he had been murdered. Nosey Nathan looked startled. "What's happened?" he demanded.

"I'm sorry to say, Nosey, that the Harbour Master-cat is dead."

Nathan was visibly shocked, and his large ears twitched dramatically. "He can't be! I spoke to him earlier this morning. How did he die?"

"It's too early to say. But tell me about your conversation with him. Was it here? And when was it?"

"It must have been about half past nine. He was out of breath. I think he'd run from the car park. He said …. 'it's a catastrophe! Sir Lancelot's yacht has been robbed. I must call the cat-police.' I think that was all. No, wait a minute, I asked him if there was anything I could do. He said ….. 'try and find out where Bouncy is and ask him to come to my office.' That was it."

"And did you find Bouncing Bert?" asked Derek.

"Yes, I got him on his mobile. He was having a cup of tea in the Brixcat Tea Rooms across the road. As a matter of fact the phone ringing startled him and he spilt his tea on his trousers. Anyway, he came straight back and went up to Brian's office."

"Brian?" queried Derek.

"Bosun Brian ...... the Harbour Master-cat. He's also the Bosun on the Brixcat Lifeboat. Well ...... he was."

Derek looked puzzled. "What's a bosun?" He looked directly at Nosey Nathan.

Nathan shrugged his shoulders. "Not sure, really," he said unhelpfully. "I'm not a seafaring cat."

"He's the cat in charge of the lifeboat when it puts out to sea, Chief," said Stanley before addressing Nathan. "I need a list, as far as you can remember, of all the cats who have gone up to the offices since eight o'clock this morning, especially any that are unknown to you."

"That'll be a bit difficult, won't it, Stan?" said Derek. "I mean how can he make a list of cats he doesn't know?"

Stanley sighed to himself. It was very difficult working with Derek sometimes. But he kept a straight face and said simply, "just list down the cats you don't know, Nosey, try to describe them and who they went to see."

"I'll do my best," said Nosey. Suddenly, without any warning, his nose began to twitch and he started to blink rapidly. A single tear from each eye slid down his cheeks, and his nose got quite wet. "Oh! I think I'm going to sneeze!" He wiped the tip of his nose with his paw. "A ….. a ……. a ……a ….. TISHOO!"

Stanley turned away in disgust as a large blob of yellowy green snot flew out of Nosey Nathan's nose and landed on Derek just above the breast pocket of his frayed grey shirt. It then slid in a slimy mess straight into the pocket.

"What do you think you're doing?" shouted Derek angrily. "I'm a cat-police officer. How dare you!"

Stanley couldn't help himself. He laughed out loud.

"That's not very nice, Stanley, laughing at my misfortune."

"I'm sorry, Chief. You're right. I was out of order."

"Oh, God," moaned Derek, when he realised exactly where the blob of snot had gone. "That's where I've got my banana sandwich. And it isn't wrapped!" He wrung his paws in anguish. "That idiot's snitty snot is going to be all mixed in with my mashed banana. That's disgusting." He thrust his paw into his breast pocket and scooped out the slimy sandwich, and threw it at Nosey Nathan. Fortunately for Nathan, his aim wasn't terribly good, and the banana snot slid down the window of the glass booth, leaving a snail-like trail glistening in the sunshine.

Nosey, meanwhile, was wiping his nose with the back of his paw, before pulling a filthy yellowy green handkerchief out of his trouser pocket. He tried to creep back into the booth.

"Just one other thing," said Stanley. "Have you left your post at any time in the last four hours?"

The security-cat hesitated. "Er .... well ... basically no." But he didn't seem terribly sure.

"What do you mean?"

"I only left to go to the toilet."

"It's important for us to know whether any cat could have sneaked up the stairs without your knowledge," pressed Stanley. "How many times did you go to the toilet?"

"About four."

"Did you go to the toilet after Bosun Brian went up to his office?"

"I can't remember. I don't make a note of the time when I go to the toilet."

"I see. Perhaps you *should* keep a record. So, you can't account for the fact that Bosun Brian obviously *did* come down the stairs and you didn't see him?"

"Perhaps you were sneezing and cleaning up your nose with that filthy rag," interrupted Derek. "Lord knows it probably takes you ages to clean a nose that size!"

Nosey Nathan shot Derek a murderous glance.

Stanley tried to take the heat out of the situation. "How many cats would you guestimate are on the first floor now?" he said softly.

Nathan thought hard for a few moments. "Guessing ..... I'd say about thirty."

At that moment they saw a huge, black Norwegian Forest cat approaching from the direction of the shops and the main part of the harbour. Stanley thought he looked quite similar to Bouncing Bert, except that he had a scruffy black and grey beard, walked normally and was wearing a captain's hat on his head.

"I think we're going to need a few more cats down here, Chief," said Stanley as they walked back up the flight of stairs. "Would you like to call the station again and ask Charlie to send down some reinforcements. We're going to have to take squintillions of statements. And, by the way, I'm glad you didn't tell the security-cat that the Harbour Master-cat must have been murdered. It's so important to keep cat-police information to ourselves. Even if we think he *was* murdered we might not want everyone to know."

"It's obvious he was murdered, Stan. Even a blind cat with a wooden leg could see that."

"Ask Apple Pie Annie to come down here too. We need her to check if there are any forensic clues. And we need to know the cause and time of death."

"We know he was alive an hour or so ago. He phoned the station. And we've seen the bruise on the back of his head. What more do we need to know?"

"We don't know that for a fact, Chief. We only know that someone *announcing himself* as the Harbour Master-cat called the station. It could have been him, or it could have been the killer, if there was one. We need to trace that phone call, confirm where it was made from. And as for the bruise we need to be sure how it was caused. At the moment we still don't know whether it was an accident or a murder."

The Same Day

"When he was growing up, he couldn't decide what he wanted to do," said Jack with a straight face. All the cats in the Crime Room were listening intently, hanging on to Jack's every word. "He couldn't choose between being a hairdresser-cat or a storyteller-cat," Jack continued. "So he tossed a coin. It was a matter of heads or tails, you see! Ha! Ha! Ha!"

There was lots of laughter and smiling faces. "Oooh, you are class, Jack" said Soppy Cynthia with the biggest smile of all. "I'm sure it's funny, but I'm not sure that I understand it."

"You are stupid Cynthia," said Cadet-Cat Studious Stephen unpleasantly. Stephen was a Blue Cream & White Devon Rex and he wore wire-framed nose glasses on account of his poor eyesight. He considered himself superior to all the other cats in the Cat-Haven Cat-Police force, and looked down on most of them. "Coins have got heads on one side and tails on the other," he said to Cynthia with contempt etched on his face. "Heads is for hairdressers and tales are what stories are. It's simple!"

There was an embarrassing silence, but fortunately the telephone on Jack's desk rang sharply. He picked it up and listened to a voice at the other end. It was Cheerful Charlie, the desk sergeant. "Jumping jellybeans!" exclaimed Jack. Then there was a long pause while Jack was listening to what Charlie had to say. "Thanks, Charlie," he said finally. "I'll get on with it." He hung up. "Listen up everyone. There's been a murder down at Brixcat Harbour. Some of us have to go there and join the Sarge and the Chief. Pamela, Stephen and you, Cyn, you three had better come, and you of course Marmy."

"What about me?" said Tammy Tickletummy indignantly. Her white fur looked clean and fresh after her shower. "I never get to go out on assignments these days. It's not fair!"

"The Chief asked that you be left in charge of the office, Tammy. It's an important job. Not just any cat could do it."

Tammy smiled. "Well, all right then."

"And what about me?" said Vacant Vincent.

"It's not really practical, Vinnie," said Jack sympathetically. "It would be too difficult to take you on an outside job, what with your problem."

Vincent looked downcast, but said bravely, "I guess you're right Jack. It could be difficult. As a matter of fact, now that you mention it, I *do* need to go for a poo now." A strained look clouded his face, and he suddenly jumped up out of his chair and rushed out of the room.

"The way he runs, hopping along like that," said Marmaduke, "he looks more like a rabbit than a cat." He laughed noisily.

"That's not very nice," said Pamela. "Don't be so cruel, Marmy."

"Tammy," said Jack, changing the subject, "can you go down to the forensic lab and tell Annie that she's needed too."

Tammy blushed slightly and smiled at Jack, happy to have been asked to do something useful.

The Same Day

S tanley and Derek found Bouncing Bert in his office studying a large chart that was spread out on his desk. His beige trousers were badly stained from the spilt tea. He jumped up from his chair, swished his bushy, black tail from side to side, and bounced towards them on the balls of his feet.

"Did you manage to contact the Harbour Master-cat's wife?" asked Stanley.

"Yes, she's on her way down here. She was pretty upset."

Stanley nodded sympathetically. "What brought us here in the first place, Bouncy, was the robbery on Sir Lancelot's yacht. Do you know anything about it?"

"No ….." Bert hesitated. "Nothing, really. Except that it happened."

"You're sure you don't know anything about it?" asked Stanley.

"Yes ….. of course I am." Again there was the faintest hesitation.

"OK. Well let's go back to the Harbour Master-cat's accident. You said you saw something out of the corner of your eye?"

"Yes."

"Sounds a bit odd to me," said Derek, interrupting. "How could you have done, considering he was in the water two metres below the level of the quay?"

"I don't know how, but I did," said Bouncing Bert aggressively. "He must have been waving his paws around."

"So, are you saying that he was still alive?" asked Stanley.

"Er .... not exactly."

"Was he groaning or miaowing at all?"

"No, I don't think so."

"What makes you think that he tripped on something?"

"He *must* have done." A look of guilt flashed across Bert's face. But it was gone in an instant. "How else could he have fallen in?" he added lamely.

"I'll need to speak to the two cats who helped you get him out of the sea. Have you found them yet?"

"Nathan told me he saw them sneaking off towards the Brixcat Tea Rooms."

"What do you mean, *sneaking off?*" asked Derek.

"Oh, that's just the way he talks. Being a security-cat he kids himself that everyone has some sort of dishonest motive, and that it's up to him to keep his eyes open for any hint of wrong doing."

"Sticking his snitty snotty nose in other people's business you mean?" said Derek, grinning hugely.

Stanley spoke next. "We'd like to use one of the offices here as a base while we look into this matter, Bouncy."

"You could use Brian's office, I suppose."

"That's what we thought," said Derek.

Stanley cringed, hoping that Derek wouldn't make the same joke again. Fortunately he didn't. "That's kind of you," replied Stanley. "And I may need to speak to you again, Bouncy. I'd be glad if you'd stay here for the rest of the afternoon."

"Not completely convincing, was he?" said Stanley once they were in Brian's office.

"That's what I thought," said Derek. "He's definitely the prime suspect. In fact I think he's guilty."

"I've told you before, Chief. It's foolish to jump to conclusions." Stanley stroked his chin thoughtfully. "I wonder if there's a connection between Bosun Brian's death and the robbery on the yacht?"

The Same Day

Jumping Jack and Marmalade Marmaduke were the first to arrive at the Harbour.

It was no surprise that Nosey Nathan was out of his glass booth in two sniffs of a cat's snout. "Can I help you?" he said.

Marmaduke poked Jack in the ribs, and spoke softly. "Just look at that nose, Jack. Do you think there's a banana in there somewhere?"

"What do you want?" said Nathan abruptly.

Jack showed his warrant card. "We're looking for Detective Sergeant Smartpants."

Nosey pointed to the staircase. "He's up there somewhere." With that he turned on his back paw and retreated to the safety of the glass booth. At least no-one can insult me if I'm alone in the booth, he thought.

"Charlie said there's been a murder," said Marmaduke when they caught up with Stanley and Derek. "Where's the victim?"

"He's in the fish warehouse, just a few hundred metres along the quay," replied Stanley, "but we don't know at the moment that it *was* murder. It might have been an accident. Are the others on the way?"

"Yes," said Jack. "Pamela, Stephen, Cynthia and Annie are in the next car. They should be here soon. What do you want us to do, Sarge?"

"I'd like the two of you to follow up on the cash and jewellery that was stolen from Sir Lancelot's yacht. I haven't got any information so you'll have to deal with it yourselves from scratch."

"I don't suppose the Harbour Master-cat told anyone who stole the stuff before he died?" said Jack.

"I really don't know. To be honest, Jack, we haven't given any time to the robbery. As I say you'll have to start from scratch."

"Come on, Marmy, let's go and interview that security-cat with the big nose."

Jack and Marmaduke left Stanley and Derek in the warehouse and retraced their steps. The security-cat seemed to be asleep. In any event he ignored Jack and Marmaduke as they approached the booth. Jack rapped on the glass door. "We need to talk to you .... out here."

Nathan huffed and puffed with annoyance. He struggled to pull up his trousers, which had slipped below his swollen stomach.

Marmaduke took out his notebook. "First of all,

for the record, we need your name."

Nathan's cheeks turned a bright scarlet in colour. "I'm known as Nosey Nathan," he said hesitantly.

"Oh my gosh!" exclaimed Marmaduke. He dropped his notebook on the ground and clutched his ribs. Although he tried hard not to laugh he was unable to stop a curious throaty sound escaping from his lips. He coughed and spluttered in his attempt to stop himself roaring with laughter. He looked at Jack, who was also trying hard not to laugh.

"If you're quite finished laughing at me I'll go back into my booth."

Marmaduke composed himself, and continued. "Just a moment, Nathan, there are a few questions. It was reported at the cat-police station that there's been a robbery on Sir Lancelot Smiles-a-Lot's boat."

"It's a bit bigger than a boat," said Nathan with a scornful curl of his lip. "It's a yacht! He's a squintillionaire, you know."

"Fine," said Marmaduke, "there's been a robbery on his *yacht*. And we believe that the Harbour Master-cat was the cat who reported it, and he also said that he knew who had done it."

"I don't know anything about that. All he told me was that there'd been a robbery."

"And now he's dead," added Jack. "So we can't get any information out of him. Who else has any information? Did he tell you who had stolen the cash and jewels from the safe?"

"No, he didn't tell me who had stolen whatever it was from the safe. He just told me that stuff *had* been stolen. And I don't know who he told about it, so I can't help you there."

Marmaduke carried on with his questions. "What's the name of his yacht?"

"It's called *The Flower of Catminster*. Maybe you don't know, Sir Lancelot's a politician-cat and he sits in the Cat-Parliament at Catminster."

"Yes, I think we know where the Cat-Parliament is, Nosey. And where is his yacht parked?"

"Are all police-cats as ignorant as you? You don't park a yacht, you moor it," said Nosey sounding superior. "It's moored in the marina, on the far side of the harbour. There's a small office over there, and it's run by the Commodore-cat of the Yacht Club. He can tell you exactly where it is, and when the robbery was reported."

"Now we're getting somewhere," said Jack.

Marmaduke nodded. "And his name is ….?"

"Ship-Shape Shane"

"Specdoinkel!" said Jack. "I might have guessed it would be something like that. OK, that'll be all for now, Nosey." He turned his back on Nathan and started to walk away. "Let's go and find Ship-Shape Shane, Marmy."

"Let's just call him Shane, Jackster. It's a lot easier to say. And can you imagine the Chief stammering over it … sh … sh…sh … sh … ship … sh …sh …

sh … sh… shape … sh … sh … sh … sh …"

Jack burst out laughing. "Don't let the Chief hear you mocking him, or you'll be in bad trouble!"

"That's reeally, reeeally, reeeeally worrying," grinned Marmaduke.

The Same Day

Jack and Marmaduke walked along the harbour road, with the harbour itself on their left. There were lots of boats, some large, some small, bobbing from side to side as the sea water lapped against the sea wall. There were shops on the other side of the road, and Jack grabbed Marmaduke's paw. "Remind me on the way back, Marmy. I promised to pop in to Brixcat Boox for my sister. She wants an ice-skating book for her birthday."

"How is Katie?" enquired Marmaduke.

"As a matter of fact, she's not very well. I think she's got cat-swine flu."

"Oh my gosh! Wish her well from me. When is she joining the cat-police by the way?"

"She starts next Monday."

"I suppose she'll have to start as a Cadet-Cat."

"Yes, she does. But between you and me the Sarge has promised to make her a Cat-Constable pretty quickly."

"That could be tricky," said Marmaduke. "Might upset a few cats."

"I'm sure the Sarge will work something out," said Jack with a grin and a huge wink.

They passed a number of kiosks offering mackerel fishing trips and others selling cockles, mussels and crab's claw sandwiches.

Marmaduke breathed in the wonderful smells of fish and salt and sea, which were carried on the breeze. "Remind *me* to stop and buy some seafood while you go into Brixcat Boox! It's ages since I had my last slice of toast and marmalade."

"Good idea," said Jack. "I'm quite hungry too."

"By the way, Jack .... you see all those boats in the middle of the harbour. Presumably they're anchored in the sand. When the tide's in, how do you get to your boat? Do you have to swim out to it?"

"Specdoinkel idea!" laughed Jack. "Well, I guess that's one way. I was here last weekend with Katie, and we parked in the main car park up the hill. As we got out of the car, there were two cats pushing a small rowing boat down the concrete ramp towards the sea. They then rowed it out to one of the boats about fifty metres away. One cat climbed onto the boat that was moored and the other one rowed back to the ramp. He pulled the boat up the ramp and put it away in a large shed. Then he walked round the quay to the far side of the harbour wall. While he was doing that his friend fired up the engine of the moored boat and took it over to the harbour wall to collect him. When I was in Cornwall recently, at a little fishing village, they had a Water Taxi in the harbour. It was a small motor boat, and took cats out to their boats that were anchored in the middle of the harbour."

As they reached the far end of the harbour they passed the full size replica of the Golden Hindcat. It was the famous ship in which Sir Francis Drakecat sailed round the world at the end of the sixteenth century with a crew of ten officer-cats and sixty sailor-cats. A little further on they came across a large wooden building. It had a huge glass window that looked out over the boats and yachts moored in the harbour. Above the entrance door, in bright blue paint, were the words **BRIXCAT YACHT CLUB**. And underneath that the words, **Commodore-cat's Office**.

Jack and Marmaduke walked in. Sitting in a huge swivel chair was a humungous black cat with a scruffy black and grey beard. He was a Norwegian Forest cat and very hairy. Perched on top of his head was a dirty off-white captain's hat, trimmed with faded gold braid. He was wearing a shirt with holes in it, under a soiled waterproof jacket.

"We're looking for Ship-Shape Shane," said Jack, taking his wallet out of his pocket. "We're the Cat-Haven Cat-Police. I'm Cat-Constable Jumping

Jack, and this is my colleague-cat, Cat-Constable Marmalade Marmaduke."

Ship-Shape Shane's shoulders shuddered and shook with glee, and he laughed out loud, clutching his ribs. "Sorry," he said, "but this isn't a caff. And we don't do toast and marmalade!"

Marmaduke's Seville Orange face went a deep shade of red. "Very funny," he said through gritted teeth. "Are you Ship-Shape Shane?"

Shane nodded.

Marmaduke glanced round the office. There were life jackets, sails, an upturned fishing boat, fishing nets, wellington boots, and loads of sailing magazines littering the floor. There was also a jumble of boat keys attached to cork balls scrunched together on a desk. "Can't say this place is ship-shape, Jack, now can we?"

"What exactly does ship-shape mean, Marmy?" said Jack with a broad grin on his face. "Doesn't it mean neat and tidy? Everything in its place?"

"Desperately untidy I'd say," replied Marmaduke.

"And the cat in the swivel chair looks pretty awful too," added Jack. "Perhaps this here Shane should be called Yucky Mucky Shane!"

It was Shane's turn to go red, and Marmaduke's turn to laugh. "Nice one, Jackster," he said, smiling. "That's reeally, reeeally, reeeeally good!"

Jack looked Shane straight in the eye. "What do you know about the robbery on Sir Lancelot's yacht?"

Shane stood up and began to pace up and down behind his desk. "Only that the safe was broken into and that cash and jewellery are missing. Sir Lancelot reported it to me, and I reported it to Bosun Brian, the Harbour Master-cat."

"When exactly was this?"

"This morning."

"Come on, Shane," said Jack. "Surely the Commodore-Cat can do better than that. I thought sailors and seafaring cats kept a log, a record of times and places. Don't you have one?"

"No," said Shane sheepishly.

"I've got another name for him, Jackster." Marmaduke's face creased into a grin. "Shambolic Shambles Shane!"

"Now, look here," said Shane sharply. "You can't just come in here and insult me. I'm an important cat round here. I'm a VIC."

Jack interrupted. He was as quick as Usain Boltcat, the fastest cat on the planet, running the 100 metres in the Cat-Olympics. "Got trouble with your breathing? Need some Vicks do you?"

The humour was lost on Shane. "Don't be ridiculous. It means I'm a Very Important Cat."

"I'm sure you are, sir," answered Jack. He turned towards Marmaduke, with his tongue pushing out his cheek. He rolled his eyeballs before continuing. "But we're important too, sir, and we would like you to treat us and our questions seriously."

"All right," said Shane, "but keep your tongues under control."

"You ought to keep your hair under control," said Marmaduke. "If you ask me, Ship-Shape Shane, you need a shower, a shampoo and a shave." Marmaduke looked pleased with himself and grinned at Jack.

Jack continued. "We need you to be more definite, Shane, about when Sir Lancelot reported the theft. Did he come here to your office?"

"I suppose it must have been about 9.30. I'd just finished my eggy toast, and was licking my fur when he came running into the office. He was very upset."

"What did he say?" asked Jack. "And try to remember his actual words."

Shane made a big thing of trying to think, scratching his head, tugging on his straggly beard, and gazing up at the ceiling. "Let me see now ......"

"We haven't got all day," said Marmaduke irritably.

"Well ...... I think he said ..... 'this is a scandal, Shane. The safe on my yacht's been broken into in the middle of the harbour where it's parked .... This marina's a shambles'."

"Shouldn't it be from where it's moored," said Marmaduke helpfully. "You *moor* boats, don't you? I would have thought you would know that!"

"I *do* know that," said Shane angrily. "I was telling you *exactly* what he said. He's a politician-cat, not a sailor-cat."

"Carry on, Shane," said Jack.

"And then he said ….." Shane paused for a moment and his face went red. "He said ….. 'this whole marina is a shambles. I blame you for this, Shane.' That's what he said. And he was very aggressive and unpleasant with it. I mean, how could it be my fault? He seems to think I've got nothing better to do than spend my time looking after his yacht! He's got a real cheek."

Jack and Marmaduke both smiled. "I take it you don't like him very much," said Marmaduke. "Did he say anything else?"

"Well, he just put the boot in a bit more. He said ….. 'you'd never get away with this sort of shambles in the Cat-Parliament!' I felt like saying ….. maybe not, but at least we don't charge outrageous expenses, like all you politician-cats do …. but of course I didn't."

"What *did* you say?"

"I asked him when he thought it had happened?"

"What did he say to that?" asked Jack

"He said that it could have been any time in the last week. He arrived here early this morning from London, and the last time he was on the yacht was last week sometime."

Marmaduke sighed. "What day was it that he was last on the yacht, Shane?"

"He didn't say."

"And presumably you didn't ask him," said Jack. It was more a statement than a question.

"No, I didn't."

"Don't you want to find out who broke into his safe and robbed him?"

"You lot are the cat-police. That's your job."

"Unless of course you already know who did it, Shane?" There was a question mark in Jack's voice, and his hazel green, unblinking eyes stared straight at Shane.

Shane hesitated, but only for a moment. "Of course I don't."

"Where exactly on the yacht is the safe?"

"I've no idea. Sir Lancelot didn't tell me and I didn't ask."

While this exchange between Jack and Ship-Shape Shane was taking place, Marmaduke walked over to the desk where there were lots of keys attached to cork balls. He turned back to face Shane. "Do you have a set of keys to Sir Lancelot's boat?"

"I have two sets," Shane replied. "Well, only one set at the moment, but I usually have two sets here."

"Why?"

"So that there is always a set in the office, and a spare set to give to any tradescats who might have jobs to do on the yacht."

"So where is the second set at the moment?"

"The painter and decorator has got it."

"Do you have his name and address?"

"No, I don't. He came in here with Sir Lancelot

a couple of weeks ago, and Sir Lancelot gave him a set of keys."

"What do you know about the death of the Harbour-Master-cat?" said Jack suddenly.

"Only that he fell in the sea and hit the back of his head on something."

"As far as I know it's only a short time since he died. Tell me, Shane, how did you know he was dead?"

"Nosey Nathan told me not very long ago. He heard it from your boss, that Detective Dimwit or something."

"I see," said Jack thoughtfully. "I don't suppose you have a list of the jewellery that was stolen?"

"No."

"Or how much cash was involved?"

"No. I'm not really interested. If you ask me it serves him right. He treats me like dirt, so believe me I'm not going to lift a claw to help him. Besides it's not my responsibility. It's your job, not mine. He just told me to report it to the Cat-Police."

"Excuse me, Shane. Didn't the Harbour Master-cat report the theft?

"I suppose so. After Sir Lancelot left, I called the Harbour Master-cat and told him to do it. It was his responsibility, not mine."

"I see you take your responsibilities seriously, Shane," interjected Marmaduke sarcastically.

"We need to speak to Sir Lancelot," said Jack. "Do you know where he is?"

"He drove straight back to London in his Rolls Royce."

"All right, Shane, can you please show us exactly where Sir Lancelot's yacht is moored."

The three cats left the Yacht Club building and walked along the quay to the edge of the harbour.

"There it is," said Shane, pointing to a huge boat moored to a floating buoy in the middle of the harbour.

"How do we get out to it?" asked Marmaduke. "We'll need to examine it."

"Why didn't you say so before we left the office?" grumbled Shane. "I'll have to go back and get the keys!"

"But how do we get out to it?" repeated Marmaduke. "Is there a taxi-boat?"

Shane's shoulders shook with laughter. "No, we can't afford luxuries like that. You'll have to row out to it, like all the other cats do. And before you ask," he said, pointing to a large shed at the far side of the harbour, "you'll be able to get a rowing boat in there. Then you'll have to drag it down to the slipway. You'll find a key to the shed on the boat key-ring."

The Same Day

"Jack!" A jet black cat, a Bombay, came running from the harbour road. "Jack!" he shouted again.

Both Jack and Marmaduke, who had been gazing at the Flower of Catminster yacht, turned round. A broad smile broke across Jack's face. "It's Little Big Ben," he said, in answer to the curious look on Marmaduke's face.

Ben was slightly out of breath when he reached Jack and Marmaduke. He and Jack high fived.

"How're you doing, Ben?" said Jack.

"Great. What are you doing here?"

"Could ask you the same question!"

"What, because you're a police-cat!" Ben laughed. "Am I under arrest?"

"Why, what've you done?"

"Wouldn't you like to know!"

"So, what're you up to? Oh, by the way, this is my mate, Marmy."

Ben shook paws with Marmaduke. "I was just delivering some clocks to the jewellers over there." He pointed towards the row of shops beyond the Golden Hindcat.

"Ben's a clock maker," said Jack to Marmaduke.

"Yeah," said Ben. "It's a family business. My grandfather started it way back. He had a contract to carry out maintenance work on Big Ben at the Cat-Parliament in London. Then he decided to make clocks himself, and moved down to Devon. Sadly he died just before I was born. That's why my Dad called me Little Big Ben. In honour of my grandfather."

"Awesome!" exclaimed Marmaduke. "So, how do you know Jack?"

"We were at school together."

Just then, Shane appeared with the keys to the Flower of Catminster, and handed them to Marmaduke. Abruptly, and without a word, Shane turned and walked back to the Yacht Club office.

"We'll have to press on, Ben. We've got to row out to that humungous yacht over there," said Jack, pointing to the Flower of Catminster. "Let's meet up for a drink soon, perhaps at the weekend if you're around. I'll give you a call."

Ben smiled. "Sounds good. Nice to have met you Marmy."

"You too," said Marmaduke.

Jack and Marmaduke strode over to the shed and put the key into its rusted lock. The battered wooden door opened with a loud creaking noise. They took a small rowing boat and two oars out onto the quay and carried it the fifty or so metres to the concrete slipway.

When they had almost reached the bottom of the slipway, Marmaduke tripped on a log that he hadn't seen, and fell forward, down the slope and into the sea.

Jack laughed. "Specdoinkel!"

Marmaduke clambered back onto dry land, his face quite red. His shoes were full of sea water and his shirt and trousers were soaking wet. "Thanks for laughing at my misfortune, Jack. I hope *you* fall into the sea next time."

"Sorry, Marmy, but it *was* funny watching you try to stay upright. Are you ok?"

"Of course I'm ok," replied Marmaduke gruffly. "Let's get this boat into the sea." He stooped to take off his shoes and roll up his trouser legs. He stepped into the shallow sea water and pulled one end of the boat towards him. Jack had been holding on to the other end of the boat and failed to let go as it slid into the sea water, which promptly covered his ankles. It was Marmaduke's turn to laugh. "Serves you right, Jack. Now *your* shoes are full of water. Now that was reeally, reeeally, reeeeally funny!"

Jack grinned. "That makes us even! Now let's

row out to the yacht. Before we do I've got a joke for you. There were two boats racing towards each other. One had twelve blue cats on it, and the other one had twelve red cats on it. They had a head-on crash and both boats turned upside down ...." Jack paused for ages.

Eventually Marmaduke said, "so what happened?"

"All twenty four cats were marooned! Ha! Ha! Ha!"

"Good one, Jack."

There were no metal supports for the oars on the rowing boat, and Jack and Marmaduke's efforts to row smoothly were made impossible. At one point they managed to make the boat tip alarmingly to one side, and they were lucky not to fall into the sea. It was obvious that neither of them would make the Great Britain Cat-Rowing Team for the 2012 Cat-Olympics in London.

When they reached the Flower of Catminster they had to climb a wooden ladder fixed to the stern in order to get on board. The cabin was locked, and Jack tried a couple of keys until he found the right one, and opened the door.

As they stepped inside Marmaduke gasped. "Oh my gosh!"

They had entered a huge lounge bar which was furnished with plush leather sofas and glass tables. There was a bar in one corner, thick carpets on the floor and expensive fabric curtains. Marmaduke whistled in admiration. "He's certainly spent plenty of money on all this, Jackster," he said. "Let's see what's through here."

Together they began to search the rest of the yacht, and soon found a room that was obviously a small cinema. There were four rows of six comfortable armchairs, which gazed at a huge cinema screen on one wall. There was a set of windows along one side only, with rolled-up blackout blinds in front of them. There was no safe to be seen anywhere.

While they walked around the boat there were loads of creaking noises, as the yacht gently bobbed from side to side. Next they came to a large cabin which had a king size double bed in it, and was presumably the master bedroom. On the starboard wall there was a built-in safe. The door hung at an angle on its hinges, and it seemed that the safe had been blown open with explosive. There were a few shards of twisted metal lying on the carpeted floor. The safe itself was completely empty.

There was a framed painting of the Golden Hindcat lying on the floor. Both Jack and Marmaduke put white cotton gloves on their paws, so that they wouldn't contaminate the crime scene while they were examining it.

"I guess this was hanging on the wall covering the safe," said Jack pointing to the painting. "Look, Marmy, there are several pawprints on it. They look quite good ones too. Can you pass me the chalk?"

Marmaduke fished a piece of white chalk out of his jacket pocket. He passed it to Jack, who drew a chalk circle round the pawprints. "We'll need to get the forensic cats down here to dust for pawprints, Marmy," he said. "Let's see what else we can find." He took out his notebook and scribbled a few notes.

There were in fact quite a number of possible pawprints that Annie and her forensic cats would be able to work on. Naturally most of them would probably belong to Sir Lancelot.

They searched the room for several minutes, but could find nothing more of interest. Their search was not helped by the winter sun, already low in the sky, which shone brightly, almost blindingly, through the starboard windows. But as they were about to leave, the brightness of the sun proved to be an advantage after all. Marmaduke's eye was caught by a flash of silver underneath one of the bedroom chairs. "Hold up, Jackster, there's something over here."

Marmaduke took a pair of tweezers out of his pocket, and crawled underneath the chair. Carefully he picked up the small object with the tweezers, and crawled back from underneath the chair. He stood up and showed the object to Jack. It was a door key, a standard Yale key, silver in colour. Carefully he deposited it in a small, clear plastic evidence bag, and put it in his pocket.

"What do you think?" said Marmaduke. "Is it possible it belongs to the thief?"

"No idea," said Jack. "We'll take it back to the station anyway."

After returning the boat keys to Shane, Jack and Marmaduke set off along the quay towards the Golden Hindcat. Shane watched them until they were out of sight.

"I must say I was surprised that Shane knew about the death of the Harbour Master-cat," said Marmaduke, as they approached Brixcat Boox.

"So was I," replied Jack. "But it'll be easy enough to check with Nosey Nathan.

The Same Day

A blue Panda car from the Cat-Haven Cat-Police car park screeched to a halt at the entrance to the harbour right next to Nosey Nathan's glass booth. In his hurry to get out of the booth to shout at the offending car, Nathan, not for the first time, caught his nose in the telephone flex and fell head first onto the ground. It didn't improve the looks of his ghastly nose! Before he could get back up on his paws, Studious Stephen, Playful Pamela, Soppy Cynthia and Apple Pie Annie were already out of the car and approaching him.

"What have we here!" exclaimed Stephen. "By the looks of it, this cat ought to change his nose." This was Stephen's weak attempt at humour, but it washed over the two female cats. Pamela bent down to help Nathan get up. "You poor cat," she said sympathetically. "Are you all right?"

Nathan looked up at her, and it was as if a bolt of lightning had struck him. Pamela was a black, smoke

59

and white Cornish Rex with long, graceful legs and large, prominent ears. She had a striking face with shades of blue and black and grey around a white mouth. Nathan thought she was the most beautiful cat he had ever seen, and he just loved her delightfully pink nose. He blushed furiously and tried to get up. "I'm fine," he said bravely. "It's very kind of you to help me up." He blushed some more, for he just couldn't stop himself from staring at her. In fact he was so overcome that he completely forgot that he had been rushing out of the booth to tell them to move their car.

At that moment, Jack and Marmaduke strolled up, licking their whiskers. They had both just polished off a crab sandwich and a potful of cockles.

"Did you park that car right here?" said Jack addressing Studious Stephen.

"Yes I did," replied Stephen.

"Well don't be an idiot, it's blocking any traffic that needs to come down here. Put it over there, where our car is parked."

Jack saw Nathan gently touching his nose. "Hello, banana bonce's nose is even more squashed than it was half an hour ago. But it hasn't got any smaller. Ha! Ha! Ha!" Pamela and Annie laughed noisily, and Cynthia did too. Nathan felt humiliated. The love of his life had just laughed at the state of his nose.

"Hey," said Jack, "why did the banana go to the doctor?"

"Tell me, Jack," said Marmaduke.

"'Cos he wasn't peeling very well! Ha! Ha! Ha!"

They all laughed again.

"Who is he, Jack?" Pamela asked, ignoring Nathan.

"He's the security-cat. They say he's got a nose for trouble. Ha! Ha! Ha!"

Pamela, Cynthia and Annie laughed again.

Jack put on a serious face. "I need to ask you a very important question, Nosey."

Pamela couldn't help herself, she spluttered with laughter. "Is that what they call him," she said in a mocking voice.

Nathan felt as small as a mouse, and he reddened once more. "What do you want?"

"I need to know if you've spoken to Shane in the last hour or so."

"As a matter of fact, I have."

"Did you mention anything about the Harbour Master-cat?"

"Yes, I told him that he was dead."

"Anything else?"

"No. That's all I know."

While Jack had been having this conversation with Nathan, Stephen had moved the car.

"Right," said Jack. "We'll all join up with the Sarge. He's in the office at the top of the stairs."

They all followed Jack. Nathan stared after them as they walked up the stairs. Sadly Pamela did not take one more look at him. He felt crushed, and struggled back into his booth. The sweetness of true love had unexpectedly arrived in his life, and just as quickly departed, to be replaced with the bitterness of rejection!

The Same Day

Stanley and Derek had set up a temporary Crime Room in the Harbour Master-cat's office. As Jack and his companions entered the office Bouncing Bert was speaking.

"I think that's a complete list, Sergeant, of all the cats who work in the offices up here."

Stanley nodded. "Thank you, Bert, you've been most helpful. Could you carry on looking for the two cats who helped you pull Bosun Brian out of the sea."

"I'll do my best, Sergeant." And with that he turned on his back paw and bounced out of the office, squeezing past Pamela and Stephen.

"Good," said Stanley. "Glad you're all here. There's a lot to be done. Marmaduke, I'd like you to divide up the offices between yourself, Pamela, Stephen and Cynthia. We need to interview all the cats in the building. First of all I suggest you go into every office and tell the cats that the Harbour Master-cat is dead. And that we don't know at this stage whether it was an accident or whether it was foul play. Make a note of any interesting reactions."

"Oooh," said Jack, interrupting, "do you mean chickens might be involved? Ha! Ha! Ha!"

There was a lot of laughter, and Cynthia laughed the loudest. "You are awful, Jack," she said, "although I don't actually know what you mean."

"Come on, Cynthia," said Stephen scornfully. "Fowls are hens and chickens, and foul play is a murder or something."

"I thought a foul play was like in a football match when one player kicks another player," said Cynthia, a bit put out.

"Well it is that as well," said Marmaduke. "Why don't you leave her alone, Stephen?"

"OK," said Stanley, realising that things were getting a bit out of control.

"Oh, oh," said Jack. "I feel a poem coming on!"

Stanley smiled and all the cats waited expectantly.

> *"When you find a cat who's died,*
> *Here is for you a simple guide.*
> *You should for him show some respect,*
> *And telling jokes you should reject.*
> *For just imagine, Jack my dear, 'twas you*
> *who died,*
> *And all your friends just asked to have your*
> *liver fried!"*

All the cats laughed, and Jack was the first. "Good one, Sarge," he said, smiling, "And I get the message!"

"OK, now let's get down to work," said Stanley. "Marmaduke, make sure to tell everyone that they are not to leave the offices until they've been interviewed. Ask all the usual questions everybody. Here's the list of cats. Off you go, Marmaduke."

Marmaduke took the list from Stanley and left the office with his three cat-companions. Jack couldn't help but notice that Cynthia was sweating profusely. He realised that she had never interviewed any cat before. He guessed that she was wondering what the 'usual questions' were. "Excuse me a second, Sarge, I just want to have a word with Cyn."

Stanley knew what was in Jack's mind, and smiled with understanding. "No worries, Jack."

Outside the office Jack took Cynthia's paw. "You'll be fine, Cyn. The first thing you have to do is tell all the cats in whatever office you go to, that the Harbour Master-cat is dead, and that you have to take a statement from everyone. Ask each cat their name, address and contact details, and ask them when they last saw the Harbour Master-cat, and if they know anything about his accident, but don't mention how he died. And while you're at it, ask them if they know anything about the robbery on the yacht. All right?"

Cynthia smiled brightly. "Thank you, Jack, I'll try my best."

* * * *

"Derek," continued Stanley, back in the office, "could you take Annie to the fish warehouse, so she can examine the body."

Derek was a bit put out. He thought that Stanley was telling him what to do. "Can't Jack take her?" he said.

"Chief, Jack doesn't know exactly where the body is, but you do."

"I suppose so," said Derek with annoyance. "Come on Annie, let's go."

As Derek turned back towards the door without looking where he was going, he bumped into Jack, who was on his way back in. "Look where you're going, Jack," he said grumpily.

"Before you go, Chief," said Stanley, "we should get Jack to update us on the yacht situation."

"Good idea, Stan," said Derek, a little happier.

When Jack had finished telling Stanley and Derek about their meeting with Ship-Shape Shane and their visit to the yacht, Derek turned to Apple Pie Annie. "Let's go, Annie," he said once more.

Apple Pie Annie twirled the set of pearls she was wearing round her neck round and round, like a hoopla. She was an American cat, a blue California Spangled breed of cat. She was a striking, slightly wild looking cat, with distinctive black spots and stripes. Her stunning eyes were almond shaped and olive green. She was on loan to the Cat-Haven Cat-Police from Catmel-by-the-Sea in California, where Stanley's cousin, Chuck Smartpants, was the sheriff. And she just loved her apple pie!

She picked up her huge black bag, which was almost too heavy to carry, full of instruments and the tools of her trade. She followed the Chief towards the office door. Derek turned round and said to Stanley, "I'll leave Annie there to get on with her work, and then I'll come back here, Stan."

"Fine, Chief."

The Same Day

J ust as Derek returned from taking Annie to the fish warehouse, a white Turkish Angora came bustling into the office, a pink scarf covering most of her face.

Stanley looked surprised. "I know you, don't I?" he said. "But I can't quite place you."

The Angora smiled a weak smile, and allowed her scarf to fall away from her face.

"Of course," said Stanley straightaway. "Your eyes! They're sooooo cool! It's Precious Gemma, isn't it?"

Gemma smiled another weak smile. She was an odd eyed Turkish Angora, one eye was gold and the other was blue. She worked as a sales assistant-cat at Cat Diamonds "R" Us. And Stanley had interviewed her during his last big case, the Mackerel Robberies.

"What are you doing here, Gemma?"

"Bosun Brian is …. sorry, was …. my husband."

"I'm so sorry," said Stanley sympathetically.

"How did he die? Bert didn't say. Just said he fell

into the sea. I can't understand it, he's …. I mean he …. was …. such a strong swimmer."

"Unfortunately he struck his head on something."

"So, it was an accident," said Gemma.

"At the moment we're not sure," said Stanley.

"Where is he? Can I see him …. his body I mean."

"Yes, of course. I'll need you to make a positive identification."

"But I thought Bert had already done that."

"It's just for the official paperwork, Gemma. Jack, would you take Gemma down to the fish warehouse."

When Jack had left the office with Gemma, Stanley searched the Harbour Master-cat's desk drawers, and then looked into the bookcase under the window.

"What are you looking for, Stan?" queried Derek.

"I wanted to see if there was a photograph of Gemma anywhere. There isn't one on his desk."

"Should there be?"

"Not necessarily, but most married male cats have a photo of their wife on their desk. Like Cheerful Charlie does back at the station."

"I used to have a photo of Ping Pong on my desk," said Derek rather sadly. "That is until that necklace problem with her brother during the Mackerel Robberies case. She never forgave me for it. But it wasn't really my fault."

Stanley saw the tears welling up in Derek's eyes, and realised that he had to change the subject.

"What did you think of Precious Gemma's reaction to the possibility that Bosun Brian's death was an accident, Chief?"

"I don't know, Stan. What did you think?"

"It was as if she was surprised, and relieved, that we didn't suggest it was murder."

"Yes, you're right, Stan. She must have been hiding something."

"She didn't really seem very upset, either."

"Maybe because she isn't upset, Stan. Maybe because she had something to do with his murder. Yes, that's it. She must be guilty."

"Now, look here, Chief, I've told you before not to jump to conclusions without any evidence."

"I hear what you say, Stan, but we'll just have to *find* the evidence."

"Remember, she wasn't here, Chief. She couldn't really have struck him over the head if she wasn't here, could she? And anyway, we still don't know whether he *was* struck on the head. We'll have to wait for Annie's report."

"I'm not completely stupid, Stan. I know we need Annie's report. Even a blind cat with a wooden leg would know that. But I still think it's obvious that it's a murder case."

The Same Day

S
tanley and Derek left the Harbour Master-cat's office and walked briskly along the quay towards the fish warehouse. Neither of them noticed that about one hundred metres behind them, they were followed by a cat who was careful to remain unseen. The fish warehouse was alive with activity, as many fishercats were unloading, sorting and checking fish that had been caught that morning.

Derek breathed in the salty smell of the sea. "All this fish is making me feel hungry, Stan."

"Me too, chief. But we haven't got time to think about eating."

They went into the small office where Annie was working on the body of Bosun Brian, with Jack looking on.

"How's it going, Annie?" asked Stanley.

"Well, I can tell you one thing, Sarge. There is a strong possibility that it wasn't an accident."

"I told you so, Stan," said Derek puffing out

his chest. "He was murdered."

"It's a bit soon to say that, Chief," said Annie cautiously. "He *might have been* hit behind the ear with a blunt instrument. There is a bruise there as we know. But I'll have to carry out a few tests in the Lab before I can confirm it."

"Interesting," murmured Stanley. "Any idea on the time of death?"

"No, not yet. I'll have a better idea back at the station. But I can say it was definitely within the last few hours."

"Well, that's certainly better than a slap in the eye with a wet fish. Thanks, Annie."

"You're welcome, Stan."

The cat who had been following Derek and Stanley along the quay had overheard every word of the conversation that had taken place in the office, including Annie's comment about the blunt instrument.

Stanley, Derek and Jack left Annie to carry on with her examination, and they went outside to search for the possible murder weapon. The mystery cat who had been listening in to their conversation with Annie was nowhere to be seen.

There were loads of empty fish boxes piled up on top of each other, and two large skips full of builder-cats' rubbish. There were several small boats turned upside down, some with fishing nets in need of repair draped over them. Bouncing Bert was standing talking to two fishercats. Stanley went over to them.

"Are these the two cats we're looking for, Bert?" he said.

"No, Sergeant. I still don't know where they are."

"Keep looking please, Bert. We really do need to speak to them."

Stanley turned back to Derek and Jack. "I think we'll have to get a team of cats down here tomorrow to search the area thoroughly – see if they can find a murder weapon, if there is one. There's too much for us to do now. And it'll be dark soon."

"What about the sea, Sarge? The murderer might have just thrown the murder weapon into the sea," said Jack.

"That is sooooo cool, Jack. Good point. Once Annie has confirmed that he was hit on the head with something, we'll get a team of divers to check it out. I can't imagine that the sea is too deep here."

"I agree," said Derek brightly. "There's not much more we can do here today. Let's go back to the station, it's freezing. And anyway, I could do with a sleep. Not only have I not had my afternoon cat-nap, my morning one was rudely interrupted!" As he said this he looked daggers at Stanley.

"Come now, Chief, we have to stay awake if we're going to solve the crime."

"Huh!" responded Derek. "Well, don't give me one of your poems about it."

Jack laughed. "That reminds me of a joke."

"Not now, Jack, please," said Stanley. "By the way, where's Precious Gemma?"

"It was a bit odd really," said Jack. "She took one look at her husband, and said 'Yes, that was the Harbour Master-cat, Bosun Brian'. She showed no emotion at all. It was as if she was examining a piece of meat for Sunday lunch. And then she said, 'is that all? I have to go, I have things to do. No doubt you'll contact me when you can release the body so I can make the funeral arrangements'. That was it. She turned her back on the dead body and left."

"All a bit suspicious," said Derek.

Stanley nodded. "Ok," he said, "let's go back to our temporary office and see how the interviews have been going."

The cat who had followed them to the fish warehouse had been standing behind a stack of fish boxes, listening in to their conversation. He stroked his chin thoughtfully.

When Stanley, Derek and Jack reached the Harbour Master-cat's office, Marmaduke, Pamela and Stephen were already there, studying their notebooks.

"Where's Cynthia?" said Derek to no cat in particular.

"She's just finishing up, Chief," said Marmaduke.

"She should be here shortly."

"As soon as she's here, we're all going back to the station. I want you all to give your notes to Greta, and ask her to arrange to have them typed up. Marmaduke, give yours to Jack. I'd like you to wait here till Annie has finished her examination of the body, and then bring her back to the station."

At that moment Bouncing Bert came bouncing into the office. He was confident that the cat-police were unaware that he had followed them to the fish warehouse, and that he had been listening in to their conversations.

"Have you found Fishercat Freddie and Mackerel Mike?" asked Stanley straightaway.

"No, as far as we know they've both gone to the Fish Market in Cod Place in Cat-Haven. And the odds are they'll both go home after that."

"Let me have their addresses and contact details, Bert."

Bouncing Bert was obviously annoyed. "Ask Nathan to get that information for you. I've got more important things to do. You do realise, Sergeant, that I'm now the official Harbour Master-cat. And that job involves a lot of responsibility." He puffed out his chest self importantly.

There was an awkward silence, which was broken by the arrival of Cynthia, tightly clutching her notebook in her paw.

"Arrange to have Fishercat Freddie and Mackerel

Mike telephone the cat-police station when you next see them," said Stanley firmly. "And don't go anywhere, Bert, we'll need to speak to you again."

On their way down the stairs, Derek had a gleam in his eyes. "Pretty quick to take over as the Harbour Master-cat, Stan, wasn't he? Too quick if you ask me. Perhaps that was his motive, getting Bosun Brian's job."

"Don't jump to conclusions, Chief," said Stanley softly.

"I hear what you say, Stan, but it's obviously him. As I've already said, there can't be any doubt about it. He's the murderer!"

The Next Day –
Thursday 8ᵗʰ December

Only rarely did Cat-Haven-on-Sea have snow. This was one of those rare days. It had been snowing heavily all through the night, and the roads and pavements were covered in a thick blanket of crisp, white snow. The air was fresh and cold. Outside the Cat-Haven Cat-Police station some kittens had built a huge snowcat. Around its neck was a red and white Cat-Haven Gooners' scarf, and perched on its head was a cat-police helmet! Much to the delight of hundreds of kittens, school had been cancelled for the day.

On his way in to the cat-police station Stanley had overheard one of the kittens, who was finishing off the snowcat, talking to his mother. The mother-cat had a very serious face and spoke sharply to her boy kitten.

"You *need* a haircut."

"I don't want one," replied the kitten.

"You *have to* have one, your hair's much too long. And this is a perfect day to have it, as you're not going to school."

"Well if I have to have one, I want to have it in school time."

"You can't miss classes in school to have a haircut."

"Why not? My hair grows in school time." The kitten winked at one of his mates.

"Maybe," said the mother-cat, "but it doesn't *all* grow in school time."

"Well, I'm not going to have *all of it off!*" The kitten turned to his mate, and with a big grin on his sweet little face said, "that told her!"

Getting to work had been a struggle for all the police-cats, but they had all made it to the cat-police station, except Playful Pamela. She had made the mistake of going outside her house early in the morning to play with the kittens who lived next door. It was a mistake because she tripped over a large snow-covered stone, and sprained her ankle. She had to be helped into the house, where she sat down on the settee with a mug of hot, sweet tea. When she telephoned the office, Stanley was already there, and was very concerned when he heard the news. He was full of sympathy, and he told Pamela to rest and get better. Pamela didn't mention the fact that she had been playing with the next door kittens.

* * * *

Tammy had arrived in the office with what seemed to be a little woolly "hat" on the end of her nose. As soon as he saw her, Marmaduke laughed.

"It's cold out there, Marmaduke," she said rather stiffly.

"Afraid your nose is going to drop off?"

"My nose is always cold in this sort of weather," replied Tammy.

"I bet it's always wet too," interrupted Jack. He and Marmaduke high fived.

Tammy wasn't to be put off however. "You've heard of ear muffs, haven't you? Well this is a nose muff!"

"What did the hat say to the scarf, Tammy?" said Jack, grinning all over his face.

"I couldn't care less," replied Tammy, swishing her tail.

"You hang around here, Tammy, and I'll go on ahead. Ha! Ha! Ha!"

Marmaduke high fived Jack, much to Tammy's disgust.

Shortly after ten o'clock Stanley was seated in Derek's office when Apple Pie Annie walked in. She had come straight from her laboratory, and was wearing a full length white coat. She had a file, thick with papers, detailing the results of the tests she had carried out on the dead body of the Harbour Master-cat. Stanley stood up immediately. "We'll go into the Crime Room, Annie. I want all our cats to hear the results of your tests."

* * * *

In the Crime Room, all the cat-constables, and cadet-cats of the Cat-Haven cat-police force were present. Except for Playful Pamela. Annie stood in front of the whiteboard so that all the cats present would be able to hear her. She took out a huge pair of blue glasses from her coat pocket, and put them on.

"Let me see now," she said, opening the file. "The Harbour Master-cat's death occurred no more than a couple of hours before I first examined the body."

"Great," said Derek, nodding at Stanley. "In other words he was still alive when the call was made to the station. Which means that he *was* the cat who phoned in."

"Probably was," corrected Stanley.

Annie took out the next sheet of paper from the folder. She plugged a memory stick into the computer which sat on a table in front of the whiteboard. After pressing a few keys, a photograph of the dead body appeared on the whiteboard. "Initially there was evidence that drowning could have been the cause of death. But as I mentioned in the fish warehouse at the harbour, there was a bruise on the back of the head. I can now confirm that the bruise was caused by a blow to the back of the head with a blunt instrument." She picked up the pointer from the desk, and placed the tip on the back of the head of the dead body. "You can see the bruise here," she said.

Studious Stephen adjusted his glasses on the bridge of his nose, and looked over the top of them at Annie. "Could it have been an accident, Annie?" he said.

Jack and Marmaduke burst out laughing. "Annie's just said he was hit on the back of the head," said Jack.

"Oh my gosh!" exclaimed Marmaduke. "What are the chances that he hit himself on the back of the head and then threw himself into the sea, Jack?"

"Specdoinkel!" said Jack. "That must be it!"

Stephen blushed a deep shade of crimson. "I was only asking for confirmation," he said.

Jack high fived Marmaduke. "I don't think *we* need confirmation that Stephen's a hopeless detective, do we Marmy?"

Cynthia leaned towards Tammy and whispered in her ear. "Even I didn't think it was an accident," she said.

"Any idea what sort of blunt instrument it might have been?" asked Stanley.

"Not really, Sarge," replied Annie. "It could have been something like a hammer, or a pole of some sort. A boathook perhaps. I don't think it would have been a stone or a brick, though. He was struck at an angle from behind. Probably by a right-pawed cat."

There was a sudden, loud miaow from Vacant Vincent, who leapt to his feet. Vincent was a Manx cat, and had no tail. Much more important than that however, was the fact that he had a bowel problem, known as Manx Syndrome. "Sorry, Sarge," he said breathlessly, as if he was in pain, "I need to go for a poo!"

"No worries," said Stanley patiently. "Off you go, Vincent."

There was no reaction from any of the other cats, because this was a regular occurrence. Vinnie the Poo, as Jumping Jack had christened him, was always leaving meetings to answer the call of nature.

Annie continued .... "As I was saying .... my original thoughts were confirmed. The blow to the head ...." Again she indicated the spot with her pointer. ".... was delivered *before* he fell or was pushed into the sea. He was definitely dead when he entered the sea, which rules out the possibility that the bruising to the head was caused by falling onto something in the water, like part of a boat for example. And one interesting fact is ...."

Again there was an interruption. Tammy Tickletummy suddenly started to wretch. She had been licking her fur and preening all the time that Annie had been speaking. Every cat in the room waited for the inevitable. And Tammy obliged. She chucked up loads of the fur she had licked into her stomach. Some cats were more likely to be sick than others. Tammy, being a long haired Siamese, was sick more than most. She was also well known amongst the police-cats of Cat-Haven for being the most fussy cat at meal times. She claimed to have a weak stomach, and it was important for her to eat the right foods. What she couldn't explain, however, was why chicken was good one day, and not good the next!

Once more Annie continued. ".... that the blow to the head was such, that without doubt there will be DNA evidence on the murder weapon."

"So that means that if we find something we think *might* be the murder weapon, we should be able to prove it one way or another?" said Jack. It was half way between a statement and a question.

"Absolutely," said Annie, nodding.

Poor little Soppy Cynthia blushed a deep red, looked over towards Stanley, and said in a quiet, squeaky voice. "I'm sorry, Sarge, I know that I ought to know, 'cos it's been explained to me before. But, sorry, I've forgotten. What exactly *is* DNA?"

Several cats laughed. The loudest laughter came from Studious Stephen.

"She's so dumb, it's almost unbelievable!" he said scornfully.

"Shut up, Stephen," said Marmaduke, jumping to Cynthia's defence. "Leave her alone. And anyway, I reckon we could all benefit from a refresher course."

"Thank you, Marmaduke," said Stanley. "It's a bit complicated to explain exactly what DNA is. Simply it's what makes every cat unique. You could say it's things inside the body that make you who you are. Do you know what genes are?"

Quick as a flash Jumping Jack broke in. "Course we do, Sarge. They're what you wear on your legs and round your bum. You've got several pairs of designer jeans yourself!" There was plenty of laughter in the Crime Room.

Marmaduke was quick to join in the fun. "Yes, Sarge, your jeans, or should I call them pants, are reeally, reeeally, reeeeally smart!" More laughter.

"Thank you boys …. *Even I* have to say that was ….. sooooo cool!" Even *more* laughter. "As I was about to say. As far as simple cats like us are concerned, genes and DNA are the same thing. Every cat in the world is unique. In other words no cat is exactly the same as another cat. What's important to us is that by examining, let's say for example a hair, we can discover what breed a cat is, like whether the cat is a Siamese, a Burmese, a Norwegian Forest cat, or whatever. More importantly, if we have a clue, like a hair on a murder weapon, Annie can run tests to establish the DNA. And remember, every cat is unique, so there can only be one cat in the whole world who has the same DNA as the DNA on the murder weapon. The hard part for us is to find a suspect whose DNA is an identical match. Once we've found that cat we can prove that he or she is the murderer. This is why a forensic scientist-cat, like Annie, is so important in all our cases."

"Yes, I think I understand," said Cynthia slowly.

Apple Pie Annie looked on with pride. She felt appreciated, and thought, not for the first time, that Stanley was a very good boss. He was always ready to support all his cats and make them feel good about themselves. He ran a happy team. She looked at her watch, which told her that it was nearly lunchtime. She was looking forward to putting her apple pie in the microwave oven in the station kitchen. This would be after the main course, which Greta was even now busily cooking. She would have hot apple pie, with lashings of Cornish vanilla ice-cream. Yum, yum! She smacked her lips at the thought.

"Is there anything else for you to report, Annie?" asked Stanley.

"No, that's all for now, Stan. I'd better be getting back to the lab."

Stanley smiled. "Thank you, Annie."

"You're welcome, Stan."

As Annie left the room, Jack spoke up. "Sarge, being as we worked late last night, can me and Marmy have the afternoon off to go to the Krazy Kats Skateboarding Arena?"

Stanley frowned. "Ordinarily, Jack, I'd say yes, but we *have* got a lot to do. And I'd like Marmaduke to set up an Incident Board after lunch. Could we perhaps compromise, and say that when Marmaduke has finished the Incident Board, you could both leave early?"

"If they can leave early, why can't I?" said Stephen. At this point Stephen even put down his book, *Chinese Cat Medicine in Western Europe Volume 1.*

Jack turned to Marmaduke. "What's more boring, Marmy, Stephen or his book?"

"Dead heat!" said Marmaduke.

Jack laughed. "That was well good, Marmy!"

"And what about me," said Tammy, despite the fact that her mouth was full of chocolate.

Stanley intervened.

"You should not spend your time complaining,
Because for all of us it is so draining.
You know with Marmaduke and Jack there
is no pain.
Despite the extra hours they work, they
don't complain.
So Tammy dear, this is what I say to you,
Spend more time working, less time feeding.
And Stephen dear, this is what I say to you,
Spend more time working, less time reading!"

At that moment Vincent pushed open the door and stepped back into the Crime Room. He was accompanied by the most delicious smell – Greta's beef stew! Every cat in the room breathed in deeply, wrinkling up their noses with pleasure. Most of them licked their lips. Stanley knew that none of them would be able to concentrate on any important business until after they had tackled the beef stew! So he took the lead. "Ok cats," he said, "let's break for lunch."

The Same Day

F ishercat Freddie, an American Black Bombay
with bright, copper-coloured eyes, was shown
in to Stanley's office by Greta the Grumbler.
Greta was a Red Classic Tabby Maine Coon, and
the cat-police station secretary and cook. She was
convinced that none of the police-cats appreciated
her. She wasn't sure which of her two roles was the
more difficult. On the one hand she was expected to
type up all the reports that were needed. This meant
that she constantly had to juggle her workload to try
and satisfy everybody. Not easy! Jack had given her
the name of Chief Assistant to the Assistant Chief!

In fact her *life* wasn't easy. She had two kittens
to look after as well. Snugsy and Bugsy. They were
twins, and simply gorgeous. But a lot of work – 'cos
they were really mischievous. They were called Snugsy
and Bugsy because soon after they were born they
curled up in a rug. And when Greta looked at them
she thought they looked as snug as a bug in a rug!

And sometimes, when her kitten-sitter didn't turn up she brought them in to the office. It was chaos! They ran around all over the cat-police station. Tammy and Pamela just loved them and kept wanting to give them cuddles. Whereas, Jack and Marmaduke encouraged them to be naughty. Stanley was very understanding, and mostly just smiled and put up with the inconvenience. Derek on the other hand was often furious and angry at the way the kittens took over, and upset the work of the cat-police.

And when it came to her other role as the cook, Greta had to put up with never ending complaints. Most of the cats were fussy, and whatever she put in front of them, there were always plenty of ungrateful miaows! The worst cat was Tammy Tickletummy. She was a real diva, and impossible to please.

"I keep asking you to get my intercom fixed, Sarge," grumbled Greta. "It's not fair that I have to walk up all those stairs every time you have a visitor. I'm working my claws to the bone. Anyway, this is Fishercat Freddie."

"When you pass his door, can you ask Chief Inspector Dimwit to come to my office," said Stanley.

"I suppose so," said Greta, with a huge sigh, as if the world was coming to an end. She swept back out of Stanley's office.

Freddie stood in the doorway, his soaking wet, heavy yellow oilskin jacket depositing droplets of rain water and melting snow onto the carpet.

Stanley came out from behind his desk. Today he was wearing a sensational outfit. His trousers were sky blue with seven little brown mice dotted around. His waistcoat was pinky-red with purple spots and cream lapels. And his bow tie. Wow! It was a stunning multi coloured patchwork of orange, blue, red, green, purple and yellow.

"Good morning, Freddie, thank you for coming in," said Stanley. "You can hang your jacket up on that peg behind the door."

Freddie took off his oilskin, hung it up and took a seat on the other side of Stanley's desk. "Nice to see you again," he said. "My sister sends you her regards."

"How is Harriet?"

"She's well. And there are no after effects from being hit on the head on Torcat Beach, I'm glad to say."

"That is sooooo cool!" said Stanley.

Chief Inspector Dimwit entered Stanley's office, and he sat down on the sofa, set against the wall behind Freddie's chair. It was one of Stanley and Derek's favourite interview techniques, one of them facing, and the other behind the cat being interviewed.

"So what can you tell us, Freddie, about the Harbour Master-cat's accident?" Stanley noticed that Derek was frowning, but he paid no attention.

"Sorry I wasn't able to wait around on Wednesday, but I had to get to the Fish Market in Cat-Haven to sell my catch."

"That's Ok, Freddie."

"I was loading my mackerel catch into my van, when I heard a shout from further down the quay. It was Bouncing Bert."

"Roughly what time was that, Freddie?"

"I didn't check my watch, but it must have been shortly after ten o'clock. Bert was shouting and waving his arms around. I wasn't sure, but I thought he was beckoning to me. So I ran towards him. He carried on shouting, and as I got closer I could only make out two words …. Brian …. and drink. He kept repeating them ….. Brian ….. drink …. Brian …. drink."

Derek interrupted. "Why would he say that Brian wanted a drink?"

"When I reached him, it became clear. What he was saying was that Brian was *in the drink*."

"I hear what you say," said Derek looking even more puzzled, "but I don't get it."

"It means he was in the sea, Chief," said Stanley with a smile. "Can I ask you to try and remember his exact words, Freddie?"

"That was it, Sergeant, 'Brian's in the drink'."

"Are you sure he didn't say that Brian had fallen into the drink?"

"No, definitely not, because I actually said to him, did he fall? And he replied, 'I don't know ….' And then he hesitated before saying … 'I guess he must have done'. At that moment Mackerel Mike came running up, shouting 'what's happened'?"

"Where had he come from?"

"That was the curious thing. I know he had been out fishing like me, but he came from the other direction, from the office direction. I didn't think anything much of it at the time. We were all too worried about Brian. Anyway I said to Mike, let's jump in. And the two of us did jump in."

"Let me just ask you something," said Stanley. "Did Bert offer to jump in as well?"

"No, he seemed quite happy for me and Mike to do it."

"Mmm," murmured Stanley to himself. "What happened in the water, Freddie?"

"Brian was lying half in the sea water and half on the deck of a derelict boat. His paws were tucked under him at an awkward angle."

Derek intervened. "What was his condition, Freddie?"

"He was dead."

"Are you sure?"

"Absolutely."

"No signs of life at all?"

"None."

"What did you and Mike do next?" queried Stanley.

"We supported him between us, and swam over to the concrete steps near to where we unload our fish catch. It was quite difficult – he was very heavy. It took us about ten minutes to swim a couple of hundred metres."

"What was Bouncing Bert doing all this time?"

"I don't know really. Me and Mike were too busy trying to get Brian out of the sea. I did hear him shout a few times, but I've no idea what he was saying. He did come down the concrete steps to help us get Brian up onto the quay."

"And then what?" asked Stanley.

"Bert said we should take Brian into the warehouse, and put him in the office there. And that's what we did. Mackerel Mike obviously didn't want to stay around, 'cos as soon as we'd put Brian's body in the office, he said, 'I can't hang around here, I've got more important things to do. I'll leave you guys to sort things out.' And off he went. I had to take my catch to the Fish Market in Cat-Haven, and as soon as possible, but it didn't seem right just to rush off like that. It seemed disrespectful."

"What happened next?"

"Bert and I stood there for a while, not saying anything to each other. After a few minutes Bert said, 'I'd better go and call the cat-police'. He asked me to stay with the body, but I explained to him that I had to get my catch offloaded and over to Cat-Haven. It wasn't as if there was anything I could do. So I went back to my boat, and the last I saw of Bert, he was bouncing along the quay towards the offices."

"Are you sure you told Bouncing Bert that you couldn't stay with the body?" It was Derek who asked the question, and Freddie had to turn round in his seat and look over his shoulder to answer."

"Yes, Inspector, I'm certain."

"It's Chief Inspector actually," said Derek proudly.

"Sorry," said Freddie.

"Just one last thing," said Stanley. Freddie turned back to face Stanley.

"Did you see Mackerel Mike again? Was he unloading his catch?"

"No, I didn't see him again that day."

"You didn't bump into him at the Fish Market?"

"No," replied Freddie, shaking his head. "There is one other thing though. When we were in the water, it seemed to me that Mike was relieved that Brian was dead. I might be wrong about that, but that's how it seemed."

"We haven't been able to contact Mackerel Mike," said Stanley. "He hasn't been back to his rented cottage since he left Brixcat Harbour early on Wednesday morning. When did you last see him, Freddie?"

"I haven't seen him since we pulled Brian out of the sea."

Stanley stroked his chin, deep in thought. "Hmmm. What can you tell us about him, Freddie. What sort of cat is he?"

"Not much really. I think he's a bit of a loner. When we pulled Brian out of the sea, it was only the second time I'd actually spoken to him. Before that I chatted to him briefly at the Fish Market once."

"What about?" asked Derek.

Freddie turned round to answer Derek. "Just fishing stuff. I can't remember exactly."

After Freddie had left the office, Derek jumped up from the sofa, and began to pace up and down. "There's a lot of suspicious behaviour, I'd say," he said. "Why was Mackerel Mike so concerned to be sure that the Harbour Master-cat was dead? Was he worried that he might still be alive, and able to identify him as the murderer? And why didn't Bouncing Bert jump into the sea to try and save him? Perhaps because he didn't want to?"

"Some interesting questions, Chief. If we believe what Fishercat Freddie has told us, then Bert lied to us."

"I hear what you say, Stan. But I don't know what you're referring to."

"Don't you remember, Chief. Bert said that he had no idea why one of them, Freddie or Mike, hadn't stayed with the body. But Freddie just told us that Bert knew that Mike had already left, and that Freddie was about to leave."

"Yes, yes, yes! I do remember that, Stan. He was obviously trying to make us suspect their motives. It all fits. Bouncing Bert's the murderer. I'm certain of it. Or it's Mackerel Mike! It's definitely one of them."

The Next Day –
Friday 9ᵗʰ December

S ir Lancelot Smiles-a-Lot stepped out of one
of the bright pink Kool 4 Kats Taxis outside
the Cat-Haven Cat-Police station. The snow
was still lying on the pavement. He was a Brown
Tortie Burmese with olive green eyes, and brown, red
and cream fur. He wore a navy blue raincoat, with
a breast pocket in which he sported a bright red silk
handkerchief. He paid the taxi driver-cat and walked
briskly into the cat-police station.

Greta the Grumbler came out from her office to
greet him. "Can I help you, sir?" she said.

"I'm Sir Lancelot Smiles-a-Lot, and I want to
see the most senior officer-cat on duty." He flashed
Greta a dazzling smile, showing his perfect, gleaming,
white teeth. He just couldn't help it. "There was a
serious robbery on my yacht two days ago in Brixcat
Harbour. My safe was broken into, and loads of cash

and expensive jewellery was stolen."

"I know who you are. I've seen you on television, with your false politician-cat's fake smiles, making false promises to the cat-public."

Sir Lancelot switched off his smile in an instant, as if he was turning off an electric light. "How dare you speak to me like that," he said, with a hard edge to his voice. "I'm a VIC."

"A what?"

"I'm a *Very Important Cat*, and *you* are a very stupid cat."

"I reckon you need some Vicks to stick up your stuck up nose! Anyway, in our cat-police lingo, a Vic is the victim of a crime. And that's all you are."

"You're riding for a fall," said Sir Lancelot viciously. "I'm in the cat-government, and I have *loads* of influence. In fact, if you're not careful I'll use my influence to have you sacked."

"Typical of a squintillionaire fat-cat politician! Abusing your position to punish hard working cats like me. I'd *never* vote for you! And personally I hope you never see whatever was stolen from your fancy boat again. I hope it stays stolen. How did you manage to buy whatever it was that was stolen anyway? Cheating on your expenses? Claiming for cleaning out your moat?"

Sir Lancelot was breathing heavily, and struggling to control himself. "I repeat, I want to see the most senior officer-cat on duty today."

"That would be Detective Chief Inspector Dimwit," said Greta. "Wait here, *sir*, and I'll go and check if he's available." Greta had to walk up the stairs yet again, for Derek Dimwit's office was on the first floor. She let out a deep miaow as she climbed the stairs. She was clearly unhappy. No more than a minute later however, she came back down the stairs. "Follow me," she said addressing Sir Lancelot. Deliberately there was no *sir* this time.

Stanley was already seated in Derek's office when Sir Lancelot was shown in by Greta. She scowled and miaowed at Sir Lancelot as she left him standing in the doorway. And she made no attempt to introduce him to the Chief or to Stanley.

Derek shook paws with Sir Lancelot and offered him a seat. "I'm Detective Chief Inspector Dimwit, and this is Detective Sergeant Smartpants," he said. "How exactly can we help you, Sir Lancelot?"

"I would have thought it was fairly obvious," said Sir Lancelot unpleasantly. "I want to know what the cat-police are doing about the robbery on my yacht."

"Our enquiries are progressing satisfactorily," said Derek.

"You sound just like a politician-cat," replied Sir Lancelot. "You haven't answered my question."

"Unfortunately we have a more important matter which is taking up most of our time" said Derek rudely. "We're investigating the murder of Bosun

Brian, the Harbour Master-cat. Stolen jewels on boats are in second place compared to a murder."

"Have you done *anything* about it?" Sir Lancelot stressed the word anything.

Derek became flustered. "We c-c-c-c-can't disclose the n-n-n-n-nature of our enquiries," he stammered. "It's standard p-p-p-p-procedure. And anyway ….."

Stanley realised that he had to help Derek out of an embarrassing situation. "I'd like to add to what Detective Chief Inspector Dimwit was saying, Sir Lancelot," he said. "We are doing our best to track down your stolen goods, as my colleague has said. However, I'm sure you will appreciate that a murder enquiry has to be our number one priority."

"We are also considering another possibility," said Derek, who had recovered his composure. "It seems possible that the theft from your boat and the murder of the Harbour Master-cat are linked."

Stanley covered his eyes with one paw. It was so frustrating. Derek never could remember not to pass on confidential cat-police information to the cat-public. But now that Derek had let the cat out of the bag Stanley had no choice but to discuss it. "That's right," he said, "we are investigating that possibility. The Harbour Master-cat made a phone call to the cat-police on Wednesday morning, in which he said that he knew who had robbed your yacht. Unfortunately he was killed before he could tell us who it was. It's an obvious possibility that he was killed *because* he knew."

"I see," said Sir Lancelot.

"There are a couple of things we *would* like to know," said Derek. "Firstly Sir Lancelot, can you confirm that you are the owner of the boat, the Flower of Catminster?"

"Of course I am." He glared angrily at Derek. "What a stupid question!"

"It's not actually a stupid question, Sir Lancelot," said Stanley interrupting. "The yacht could be owned by a company, a business that you have an interest in for example." Stanley had moved to a chair directly behind the politician-cat, so that he would have to turn round to answer his questions.

Sir Lancelot was forced to swivel round in his chair. He immediately went red in the face. "Well .... er .... well .... it is .... er .... officially owned by one of my companies."

"Not such a stupid question after all, was it?" said Derek, grinning from ear to ear. "So who does own the boat?"

Sir Lancelot was about to turn round to face Derek, but Stanley was the next to speak. "Can we please have the name of the company, Sir Lancelot?"

Sir Lancelot hesitated for a moment before answering. "It's called Parties 4 Top Cats."

Chief Inspector Derek Dimwit laughed. "You need a humungous luxury boat to arrange parties, do you? Rent it out to other politician-cats do you? I suppose it goes down as expenses on your Cat-Tax Return?"

Sir Lancelot blushed some more.

"We also need to have a complete list of everything that has been stolen," said Stanley. "All we know at the moment is that it was some cash and some jewels. We need descriptions of the jewels, and of course exactly how much cash was taken."

"Exactly," added Derek. "If you want some action, you should have provided us with that information already! We can't be expected to find stuff we don't know anything about, can we?" Derek sat back with a satisfied smirk on his simple, black and white face. He tweaked his whiskers with his paw.

Stanley wanted to laugh, but he kept a straight face and asked, "do you have a list with you of what was stolen?"

Sir Lancelot looked sheepish."Well no," he said quietly. "I'll e-mail you a list later on today."

"Do you have any photographs of the various pieces of jewellery?" said Stanley.

"Yes, as a matter of fact I do. I'll make sure you get them."

"Were they insured, Sir Lancelot?" asked Derek.

"Of course they're insured, you idiot. They cost a lot of money."

"I'll bet!" said Derek.

"We'd be most grateful, Sir Lancelot," interrupted Stanley, "if you would not address the senior officer-cat of the Cat-Haven Cat-Police in that insulting manner."

"Quite right, Stan. Thank you," said Derek.

"How much were these jewels insured for, Sir Lancelot?" said Stanley.

Derek and Stanley's interview technique was working perfectly. Sir Lancelot didn't know where to look, and seemed completely confused and ill at ease. He even blushed. "I'm not sure," he said unconvincingly.

"Roughly will do, sir," said Stanley.

"I think it's about twenty thousand cat-euros."

"Wow!" said Derek. "Twenty thousand cat-euros for a few fancy jewels! Nice one. So if we can't find them, you get twenty thousand cat-euros?"

Sir Lancelot twisted round in his chair once more. "I suppose so," he said. Again he blushed.

"I guess it's better than a slap in the eye with a wet fish," said Stanley, stroking his chin. "Mmm." He sat quite still in his chair, thinking. After a minute of complete silence, during which Stanley spent the whole time licking his fur, Derek coughed loudly.

"Ahem, Stan. Shall we carry on?" But Stanley would not be rushed, although he stopped preening. "I suppose so, Chief. Sir Lancelot, how many cats have a set of keys to your yacht?"

Sir Lancelot was now facing Stanley. He thought for a few moments. "I have two sets," he said. "My personal assistant has one, my private secretary-cat in the Cat-House of Commons has one, and of course Ship-Shape Shane has two."

"Why does he have two sets of keys?" asked Stanley.

"Yes, why does he have two sets of keys?" echoed Derek.

Sir Lancelot hesitated. He was unsure who to answer! At last he addressed Stanley. "One is kept permanently in the Commodore-cat's office at the harbour, and the other is a spare for tradescats or any cat who has to carry out work on the yacht."

Derek continued. "Who would have been the last cat to have had the spare keys?"

"Willy Splish," said Sir Lancelot without hesitation. "He had it the week before last. As a matter of fact I have his card here." He fished into his jacket pocket and came out with a dog-eared business card. He handed it to Derek, who laid it down on the desk in front of him and studied it carefully. He then read it out loud.

SPLASH SPLOSH
Painters and Decorators

**Paintbrush House,
16 Decorators Lane, Cat-Haven-on-Sea
Telephone & Fax: Cat-Haven 7834
E-mail: splashsplosh@yahoocat.co.uk**

Willy Splish
Manager-Cat

*"You splash out the cash
We splosh on the paint!"*

"Curious name for a decorating company," said Stanley. "Does he still have the keys?"

"Yes he does. Actually I was a bit surprised when Shane told me that he hadn't returned them. He should have done."

"Why did Willy Splish have the keys to your yacht, Sir Lancelot?" asked Derek.

"I would have thought it was obvious, Inspector," replied Sir Lancelot scornfully. "To do a painting and decorating job of course. He finished the job ten days ago."

"It's Chief Inspector actually, as you already know. Are you being deliberately insulting? And please do me the courtesy of looking at me when you speak to me! It won't do you any good to be rude to the senior office-cat of the Cat-Haven Cat-Police. You might get away with that sort of behaviour in the Cat-House of Commons, but not here."

"Might I suggest, Chief," said Stanley quickly, trying to avoid a nasty scene, "that we ask Jack and Marmaduke to come in so that they can update Sir Lancelot on their enquiries?"

"Good idea, Stan." Derek buzzed the Crime Room on his intercom. This one *was* working.

Playful Pamela answered. "Hello, Chief, what can I do for you," she said brightly.

"Hi Pamela, could you please ask Jack and Marmaduke to come to my office as soon as possible. And ask them to bring in their notebooks on the Flower of Catminster case. Thanks."

* * * *

Two minutes later Jack and Marmaduke entered Derek Dimwit's office without knocking.

Derek was annoyed, but didn't react in front of his visitor. Instead he said, "Sir Lancelot, these are two of my best officer-cats, Cat-Constable Jumping Jack and Cat-Constable Marmalade Marmaduke. They have been assigned to the case of the robbery on your yacht. Jack, would you please give Sir Lancelot an update on the case."

Without any warning, Jack suddenly threw his notebook to Marmaduke, and jumped up onto the top of Derek's tall bookcase with one huge leap. He looked down at Marmaduke. "See, Marmy, I told you I could do it!"

"Oh my gosh!" said Marmaduke. "So you did, Jackster That's reeally, reeeally, reeeeally awesome!"

"Jack, please treat this matter seriously," said Stanley, although inwardly he was smiling. The self important Sir Lancelot needed to be taken down a peg. "And come down off the bookcase."

Jack grinned a huge grin as he jumped back down, took back his notebook from Marmaduke, and stood next to Derek's desk. "What would you like to know, Sarge?"

Stanley was concerned that they did not give too much information away. "Tell Sir Lancelot what happened when you interviewed the Commodore-cat, Jack."

* * * *

Jack referred to his notebook on numerous occasions as he gave his account of the interview with Ship-Shape Shane, and their subsequent visit to the yacht. He didn't mention the yale key they had found in the bedroom.

"Is that all?" said Sir Lancelot, obviously unhappy at the lack of progress. "I don't think you cats are taking the theft from my yacht at all seriously."

"We are, sir," said Stanley.

"Well it's not good enough. Some cats are more important than others. And believe me there is no cat in Cat-Haven at this moment who is more important than me!"

"Look here," said Derek, "I've had enough of your complaints. We've given your boat a case number. What more do you want?"

Sir Lancelot stood up and swished his tail angrily. He glared at Derek. "It's not a boat, you moron, it's a yacht. I'll see to it that you are put in your place, *Chief* Inspector. You'll regret you tangled with Sir Lancelot Smiles-a-Lot. I'm going to inform the mayor of your behaviour, and insist that he disciplines you."

"Specdoinkel! Ha! Ha! Ha!" laughed Jack. He gave Marmaduke a high five.

"That's reeally, reeeally, reeeeally worrying," said Marmaduke.

Stanley smiled.

"That won't do you much good," smirked Derek. "The Mayor is my cousin, and he gave me the job. So, stick that up your false teeth!"

The Next Week – Monday 12ᵗʰ December

Stanley left his house early to go to the gym. It wasn't something he did on a regular day of the week or anything like that. He just went when he felt he wanted to have a physical work out. This was one such morning.

Straight after the end of his workout he felt really fit. But he also felt ravenously hungry, and so he went into Cat-Tucky Fried Chicken. Before he was half way through his second chicken leg, there was a bleep on his personal mobile. It was Pretty Peaches returning his earlier text.

Yes, can meet u later. When n where?

Stanley tapped out his reply.

Let's go 2 the Chop Suey-Cat Chinese restaurant. Pick u up at 8.

Stanley took another mouthful of his chicken and

stuffed a few more chips into his mouth, only to be interrupted by another bleep. This time on his office mobile. He always carried two mobile phones with him. It meant that he was able to keep business and personal matters separate. And deep down he thought it was sooooo cool too. It was Jumping Jack with an important message.

Annie says boathook result this afternoon

Late on Friday afternoon one of the divers who was searching the sea bed in Brixcat, had discovered a boathook, weighted down with an old and very rusty anchor. The boathook had what looked like blood on it, and it was brought back to the cat-police station, and given to Annie to examine.

Stanley was anxious to know the result of Annie's examination, and he wolfed down the last of his chicken, licked his whiskers, and drained his cup of Pepsi-Cat. He then hurried back to the cat-police station.

He called Jack into his office. "What's the situation, Jack?"

"Annie said she should have some information for us later this afternoon."

"I don't suppose we have any idea where the boathook and anchor came from, or which boat they were off?"

"No," replied Jack. "At this stage we don't know

if both things came from the same boat. I've taken a photo of them and Katie's organising getting some copies printed. I thought perhaps a couple of us could go down to Brixcat Harbour with the photos and see what we can find out."

"Smart work, Jack. We'll send Katie and Pamela. Anything else?"

"Yes, it turns out that Precious Gemma took out an insurance policy on the Harbour Master-cat's life. On his death she's due to come into a large sum of money."

"Interesting," said Stanley. "Do we know how much she's going to get?"

"Two hundred thousand cat-euros!"

"Miiii...aow!" exclaimed Stanley, raising his eyebrows. "Better than a slap in the eye with a wet fish! Definitely a nice little payout. Any idea when she took it out?"

"Only two months ago," responded Jack.

"I would say that makes her a pretty solid suspect, wouldn't you, Jack?"

"I agree, Sarge. A definite suspect. Shall I ask Marmaduke to update the Incident Board?"

"Good idea, Jack. Any news on Mackerel Mike?"

"No, he's still missing. No-one's seen him since last Wednesday, just after Bosun Brian was found dead."

"Has the list of the stuff stolen from Sir Lancelot's yacht been printed up?"

"Yes, Katie did that this morning." Suddenly Jack jumped up and down, opening and closing his paws, as if he was trying to catch a butterfly. Then he jumped into the air, and did a backward somersault. "I wonder," he said excitedly. "Do you think there could be a connection, Sarge? Both the cash and jewels from the yacht, and Mackerel Mike, disappearing at the same time."

"Interesting thought, Jack," said Stanley, stroking his chin. In the meantime I'd like you and Marmaduke to go and see that decorator-cat, Willy Splish. Go down to his office early tomorrow morning. Can you tell everyone that I want to have a meeting in the Crime Room at ten o'clock sharp tomorrow morning. You and Marmaduke should be back from Willy Splish's place in time. By the way, how's Katie getting on?"

"Just fine, Sarge," said Jack smiling. "Like a professional skater at an ice rink!"

Skatie Katie was Jack's sister, an American Wirehair with frizzy fur. Whilst Jack's tabby colouring was black and grey, Katie's was brown and grey. But they both had the same white blaze between the eyes and round the nose and mouth. She had won the Figure Skating Gold Medal at the Winter Cat-Olympics in Bournemouth last year. She had been the resident skating coach at the Cat-Haven Ice Rink, until a couple of months ago. She had seriously damaged an ankle playing a Super Mario Power Tennis game on her Wii with Jack. She had jumped too enthusiastically to play a shot, and had hurled herself off her paws, and crashed into a glass table. The table shattered and a super sharp shard of glass had embedded itself in her ankle. Jack had taken her to the A & E Department of Torcat Hospital with the sliver of glass still in her ankle. The doctor-cat who examined her decided that she needed an operation – the glass had gone in so deep that it had severed one of the tendons. Sadly it meant that Skatie Katie would never be able to skate again in competition, and would even find it almost impossible to carry on with her coaching job.

After many chats with Jack, and one with Stanley, Katie had decided to apply for an upcoming job with the Cat-Haven Cat-Police. And she had got the job. This was now the start of her first week.

Later that afternoon, Apple Pie Annie breezed into Stanley's office.

"Hey, Stan, how you doing?" she said with a bright smile on her face.

"I'm good Annie. How are you?"

"Fine, Stan, fine."

Stanley got up from his chair as Annie came into the room.

"Hey, Stan, I just love those pants!"

Stanley smiled.

"They're great. In fact ..." she said with a wicked smile on her face, "... they're sooooo cool!"

Derek, who was already sitting in Stanley's office, looked on with a sad expression on his black and white face. The truth was that he was jealous of Stanley's pants. Stanley had so many different trousers, and all of them were admired by the female cats. Apple Pie Annie had never made a nice comment about Derek's trousers. In fact he sometimes thought that she didn't really notice him at all. Although Derek was the boss, he felt that Annie treated Stanley as if *he* was the boss. And what made things worse was the fact that since his failed relationship with Ping Pong, he had become sweet on Annie. He sighed a deep sigh, which went unnoticed by Annie and Stanley.

Annie sat down, and Stanley returned to his office chair. "I've got some interesting news for you," she said. "The blood and hairs on the sharp end of the boathook are an exact match with Bosun Brian's DNA. So I can confirm that it *is* the murder weapon."

"Excellent. Are there any clues? Any pawprints?"

"There are two pawprints, one is a bit blurred but the other one is perfect."

"Good news! That is sooooo cool!" Stanley grinned, and Annie chuckled. "What about the anchor?" Stanley asked. "Did that have blood on it?

"There was a small amount, yes, but it wasn't Brian's blood. It's a different DNA."

"I wonder if it could be the murderer's blood. I don't suppose you're able to say whether the blood was fresh or whether it had been there for a long time?"

Annie smiled. "Hold up, Stan. Gimme a chance!

There is a test I can carry out, but it will take a bit of time."

"Sorry, Annie, I didn't mean to press you."

"No problem, Stan. One interesting thing about the boathook is that it's very distinctive, in more ways than one. The handle isn't completely smooth – it's got a cut-out for a cat's paw. It's also got a reference number painted on it **FCBH03**

"**FCBH03**," repeated Stanley. "What can that mean? Any ideas, Annie?"

"No, sorry Stan, no idea at all."

"Mmm. Anyway, thanks for that, Annie. It's a lead, and most importantly we've found the murder weapon."

The Same Day

S tanley had arranged to take his special friend, Pretty Peaches, out to dinner. He collected her from her fifth floor apartment at Cat-Haven Towers on the sea front. He was wearing what he called his gold and silver outfit – a pale, but shiny, gold shirt and shiny silver trousers with wafer thin blue stripes. He almost always wore a bow tie, and this one was a plain blue which matched the stripes on his trousers. As usual his black shoes were highly polished. And of course he was wearing his favourite aftershave, Brut for Cats. Despite the winter chill he didn't wear a coat.

Pretty Peaches opened the door of her apartment. She was a beautiful cat, a peach marbled Australian Mist, with a gorgeous peach coloured face and deep gold, almond shaped eyes. She was wearing a stunning blue dress with sparkling sequins and fancy whatnots.

"You look gorgeous," said Stanley, beaming all over his face.

"Well, thank you, Stanley," replied Peaches with a twinkle in her eye. "You don't look bad yourself!" She embraced him warmly. "You smell good too!" she said.

They were going to the Chop Suey-Cat Chinese restaurant, which was situated in Torcat Road, the main street in Cat-Haven that led down to the sea from the level crossing. It was in the middle of fish and chip shops, souvenir shops and amusement arcades.

Stanley had booked Kool 4 Kats Taxis, and he and Peaches stepped out of one of their seriously pink cabs. There was snow on the ground and it was bitterly cold, the wind blowing off the sea, cutting through them like a knife through warm butter. They hurried into the restaurant, where they were greeted by a Chocolate Point Siamese cat who had a thin white body, large ears, bright blue eyes and a triangle-shaped face with a pointed chin. He smiled a toothless smile and bowed politely.

"Good evening, Chief Inspector," he said. "Chop Suey Charlie at your service. Let me show you to one of our special table." He held out his right paw, and guided Stanley and Peaches to the far side of the restaurant. As they took their seats a waiter-cat approached their table. As he got closer both Stanley and Peaches wrinkled up their noses. There was a horribly strong and unpleasant smell.

"Solly, solly, Chief Inspector. This my part-time waiter-cat he usually work on farm cleaning house of pigs and chickens. This why he smell so bad. We call him Hing Hong Big Pong."

"I'm not surprised," said Stanley under his breath.

"But he bling you lice clackers for your enjoyment."

The waiter-cat put a plate of rice crackers on their table. As he turned away Stanley and Peaches were treated to a fresh whiff of his body smell.

I depart now and return with menu," said Chop Suey Charlie. The same toothless smile crossed his face once more.

"Sounds like a railway timetable, doesn't he?" grinned Stanley after Charlie had turned away.

What they didn't see was that as soon as he had turned his back on them Charlie automatically switched off his smile, as if he was an electric kettle that had just come to the boil!

"Doesn't he know that you're a Sergeant, Stanley?" asked Peaches as they tucked into the rice crackers.

"I'm sure he does," said Stanley. "I think it's his way of buttering me up. In my view he's a very false cat. He only smiles when he thinks it does him some good." A bit like Sir Lancelot Smiles-a-Lot, thought Stanley.

Suddenly there was a loud shout from the other side of the restaurant. A group of six Chinese cats were playing dice, and an argument had started.

One of the cats got up from the table and attacked one of his companions.

"You cheat!" screamed the attacker as he grabbed the other Chinese cat by the throat. "I kill you! Me Hong Po Flied Lice. No cat cheat with Hong Po Flied Lice. You clooked Chinese cat. You tly steal my money. You bling shame to Chinese dice table. I kill you!" Hong Po's face was flushed with rage and his claws dug into his companion's face, drawing blood. The other dice players tried to drag Hong Po away, but he screamed even louder. "I kill you, Sweet and Sour Wing Wang. You no sweet, you all sour!"

"You no call me cheat, you brind cat. I no cheat. You as brind as a Chinese bat hanging upside down."

Hong Po Fried Rice swung a paw at Sweet and Sour Wing Wang and punched him clean on the nose.

One of the other dice-playing cats grabbed Hong Po by the ear and pulled him away from Wing Wang. Blood was streaming from Wing Wang's nose and he tried to stop the flow with a bright white napkin. It was soon covered in blood.

By this point Stanley had got up from his table and gone over to the fighting cats. "I'm Sergeant Smartpants of the Cat-Haven Cat-Police." It seemed the right time for a poem, and he spent just a few seconds composing one.

> *"I beg you both to hear me say,*
> *That to fight does spoil your day.*

So put your quarrel on one side,
And swallow down your pride.
For if you both do shake the paw,
You can stay friends and play some more!"

Hong Po seemed to have calmed down, although he was still breathing heavily. He looked at Wing Wang and saw in his eyes that he hadn't really cheated. He held out his paw, and after a few seconds of thought Wing Wang, whose nose had stopped bleeding, grasped it firmly. They were friends again!

"You velly crever cat Sergeant Smartpants," said Hong Po. "You make us fliends again. And you have velly smart pants too!"

"Well done, Stanley," said Peaches after he had returned to their table. "You've certainly got a magic touch."

"I don't know about that, but at least they've stopped fighting."

While Stanley had been over by the dice players another of the waiter-cats had brought some menus, and they set about deciding what to eat. After studying the menu for a while Stanley looked up.

"Have you chosen, Peaches?"

"I can't decide, Stanley. Why don't *you* choose."

"Ok," said Stanley, "let's start with Spring Rolls, and then we'll have some Aromatic Crispy Duck."

"Sounds good," said Peaches.

"I just love their Cat-Haven Special Chop Suey. Shall we have that as well?"

"Is that the one with prawns, chicken and pork and mixed vegetables?"

"Absolutely," said Stanley licking his whiskers. He started preening himself in anticipation. "It's sooooo cool," he said. "And we'll have some Tiger-Cat beer of course!"

The waiter-cat came over to their table to take their order. He looked very similar to Chop Suey Charlie. "Me Yong Kong Kevin," he said with a sickly smile, just like Charlie's. "You want order?"

As Stanley went through their order Kevin repeated their choices; "Yes prease, Spling Lolls ..... Alomatic Clispy Duck .... Special Chop Suey, velly velly good choice." He waited expectantly for Stanley to continue with his order, but it seemed that he had finished. "You want egg flied lice?" he asked with another sickly smile.

"Yes, all right," said Stanley, "and Tiger-Cat beer for both of us."

Yong Kong Kevin turned away, and left their table.

When he had gone Stanley said, "Peaches, how well do you know Precious Gemma?"

"I don't know her that well really. We work together, that's all. I've never been out with her for a drink or a meal, or to any social event. And we're pretty busy at Cat Diamonds 'R' Us, so there's not much time to gossip. Why do you ask?"

"Well, you know her husband, the Harbour Master-cat at Brixcat, was killed a few days ago ...." Peaches nodded. "What you won't know, and at the moment this is confidential information, is that it was murder."

"Miaow!" squeaked Peaches, clearly shocked.

"I was wondering about Gemma's behaviour since last Wednesday. Has she been in to work?"

"She left the shop early on Wednesday. In fact it was about lunchtime. But she didn't say why she was going. Presumably she got a call to go to Brixcat harbour. It wasn't until Thursday morning that we found out about her husband."

"Was she at work on Thursday?"

"Oh, yes, all day. She must have told Diamond Lil about it, but she didn't mention it to the rest of us."

"Curious. So how did you find out?"

"Lil told us when Gemma went out for lunch."

"What exactly did Lil say?"

"Shortly after Gemma went to lunch, Lil called me in to her office. She told me that Bosun Brian was dead, and that she had told Gemma that she didn't need to be at work – the rest of us would manage. She then said that Gemma told her that she preferred to be at work. Lil thought that Gemma was taking it very calmly, that perhaps she hadn't yet realised what exactly had happened. She said that Gemma seemed really casual, matter of fact about it all. As if she was talking about someone she hardly knew."

"Mmm," murmured Stanley. "And has she been at work ever since it happened?"

"No, she hasn't been in since Thursday. Apparently she rang in early on Friday morning and told Lil that she thought it better to have some time off."

"What conversations if any did you have with her about it?"

"Just the one, really. That first afternoon, Thursday, when she came back from lunch, I mentioned that Lil had told me what had happened. And I said how sorry I was, and asked her if there was anything I could do. She said she was fine and there was nothing she needed. She was quite cold about it. It was as if she wasn't terribly interested. She made it obvious that she didn't want to talk about it, so we all left it to her to bring up the subject if she wanted to. But she didn't. Not even once. I thought it was rather odd."

"Did she get on with her husband as far as you know?"

"You know, I don't remember her ever mentioning him. I only knew she was married because Lil mentioned it one time. I never saw her wearing a wedding ring. I didn't even know his name was Brian, or what job he did, or anything. She kept that part of her life to herself. That's all I can tell you, Stan." Suddenly Peaches chuckled.

"What?" said Stanley.

Peaches grinned. "Completely the opposite to me," she said. "I'm always talking about you, and dropping your name into conversations."

"Always good, I hope," said Stanley, smiling.

"Of course, Detective Sergeant," she replied with a perfectly straight face. She smoothly changed the subject. "Ooh look," she said. "Here come our spring rolls!"

The Next Day –
Tuesday 13ᵗʰ December

I t was five minutes to eight in the morning, and Jack and Marmaduke sat in their Panda car outside Paintbrush House in Decorators Lane. They were waiting for Willy Splish to arrive at his office. More accurately they were *hoping* he would come to his office. It was quite possible that he would not come into his office at all, but go straight from home to whatever job he was working on. It was a bone chillingly cold morning. There had been a severe frost overnight, and Jack and Marmaduke had spent nearly ten minutes scraping the frost from the car windows. There wasn't a garage at the Cat-Haven Cat-Police car park, and all the cat-police cars were left in the open air overnight. They both wore heavy overcoats, thick woolly scarves and blue woolly hats with the words 'Cat-Haven Cat-Police' picked out in white letters. Their paws were covered with huge, warm gloves.

* * * *

They had been sitting in their car for fifteen minutes getting colder and colder.

"I think we'll turn the engine on, Marmy, and turn the heater up high. See if we can warm up a bit," said Jack, as a sudden shiver made him grit his teeth. Less than a minute later, a white, frost covered van, sign written **Splash Splosh Painters & Decorators,** pulled up in front of them. A tall, skinny cat climbed out and slammed the van door behind him. His legs were as skinny as a couple of stringless beans. He was a Maine Coon, and as far as Jack and Marmaduke could tell, he was black in colour. He walked swiftly to the front door of Paintbrush House. The door was badly damaged, and it looked like it had been broken into. The lock appeared to be brand new. The skinny cat took a key from his coat pocket and thrust it into the lock. Jack and Marmaduke were already out of their Panda car.

"Are you Willy Splish?" said Marmaduke in a loud voice. The tall, skinny cat turned round as he pushed his office door open.

"Who wants to know?" he said unpleasantly, not noticing their woolly hats.

"Cat-Constable Marmalade Marmaduke of the Cat-Haven Cat-Police, and my colleague-cat," said Marmaduke, indicating Jack, "Cat-Constable Jumping Jack. I take it you *are* Willy Splish. We'd like a few words with you, sir."

"I haven't got time," replied the skinny cat.

"We're not really asking you, sir," said Marmaduke.

"Well make it quick," said Willy Splish, "it's freezing out here."

"In your office please, Mr Splish. We're not going to stand out in the street. Unless of course you would prefer to come back to the Cat-Haven Cat-Police station with us."

"You'd better come in then," said Willy Splish grudgingly.

Jack and Marmaduke followed Willy Splish down a dingy corridor and into a small room, dominated by an old and battered wooden desk with a straight backed, fixed leg chair behind it. The only other furniture in the room was a filing cabinet and two grey, "doctor's waiting room type", plastic chairs. There was no carpet on the floor, just bare floorboards, and the room certainly hadn't seen so much as a solitary splash of paint in years.

"Can I see your identification please?" said Willy Splish. Jack and Marmaduke produced their warrant cards, which Willy studied carefully. "Ok, you might as well sit down. I have to go out soon, so I hope this won't take long."

Marmaduke looked at Jack, who nodded and said, "we understand that you recently did some work on Sir Lancelot Smiles-a-Lot's yacht. Can you confirm when that was?"

"I had some work there a couple of weeks ago,"

"What job were you doing?"

"I was painting the ceiling and the walls in the main lounge, where the bar is."

"I thought I could smell paint when we were there, Jack," said Marmaduke. "Did you have any painting to do in the master bedroom?"

"No."

"Did you go into the master bedroom?"

"No. I had no reason to."

"We understand," said Jack, "that you still have the key to Sir Lancelot's yacht, even though you've finished the job."

"That's right," replied Willy, looking a little nervous.

"Why?" asked Marmaduke.

"He hasn't paid me yet. I always keep a client's key until he's paid his bill. It's a sort of insurance policy."

Pointedly, Marmaduke looked at Jack and raised his bushy orange eyebrows. "What do you mean exactly by a sort of insurance policy, Mr Splish?"

Again Willy Splish looked nervous. "Well er ...." he stumbled, "it just is," he added lamely.

Jack took up the questioning. He and Marmaduke had watched Stanley and Derek's interview techniques, and tried to copy them. "Do you mean, so that you can break in to your client's premises to take your payment in kind?"

"Of course not."

"To steal from your client?" said Marmaduke.

"Of course not," repeated Willy Splish. He went

red in the face. "How dare you suggest such a thing! That's a slanderous statement. It's disgraceful. I'm going to report you to the cat-police!"

"We are the cat-police, sir," said Jack quietly.

"Well to your superior officer, then," said Willy.

"It's normal cat-police procedure to accuse the suspect of committing the crime," said Marmaduke.

"What crime? What suspect?"

Jack took over. "As you know, cash and jewels have been stolen from the safe on Sir Lancelot's yacht. We'd like to know if *you* are the thief."

"I didn't know Sir Lancelot had been robbed. It's nothing to do with me."

Marmaduke abruptly changed the direction of their questioning. "Before Sir Lancelot, who was the last client who failed to pay you for the work you had done?"

Without thinking, Willy Splish blurted out, "Lollipop Lola at the Kitty Kat Ice Cream Parlour." The moment the words had come out of his mouth, he regretted it. "Well, not exactly," he added quickly. "There was a bit of a dispute."

"Did you keep her key?" asked Jack bluntly.

"Well ..... I suppose so."

"You *suppose so,*" repeated Jack in amazement.

"I think we can take that ... " said Marmaduke, fishing in his trouser pocket and bringing out a salt cellar, "... with a pinch of salt!" He turned the salt cellar upside down and sprinkled some salt on his paw, and then threw it over his left shoulder. "Either you did, or you didn't keep her key!" he added.

"Ok, so I did keep it," said Willy sullenly.

It was Jack's turn once more. "Did you steal anything from the Kitty Kat Ice Cream Parlour?"

"No, I did not," said Willy, although his face turned a pale shade of pink, and he did not make eye contact with either Jack or Marmaduke.

"Did you do decorating work at the Ice Cream Parlour?" asked Jack.

"Yes."

"And when was that?" said Marmaduke.

"About a month ago." Willy scratched his nose with one of his claws. His right paw had streaks of white paint on it.

"Am I right in thinking, Mr Splish," said Jack, "from the paint on your paw that you're a right-pawed cat?"

"Correct," said Willy.

Marmaduke continued. "What was the nature of your dispute with Lollipop Lola?"

Willy turned his head away at an angle of ninety degrees, and stared out of the snow encrusted window. He remained motionless for what seemed like several minutes, as if deep in thought, before turning his head back to face Marmaduke and Jack. "She complained that my work was sub-standard. I disagreed."

"And?" queried Jack.

"She refused to pay my invoice in full."

Quick as a flash, Marmaduke responded. "So, you thought that with her key, you could sneak back into her premises and take what you considered was owing to you?"

Willy Splish looked extremely uncomfortable, and said nothing.

Jack abruptly changed the subject. "How's business Mr Splish?" he asked.

Willy Splish hesitated for several seconds. "It's all right," he said eventually.

Suddenly Jack stood up. "We'd like to have a look round your premises, Mr Splish."

"Do you have a search warrant?"

"Why on earth would we need a search warrant? Have you got something to hide?"

Willy Splish took a deep breath. "Isn't it normal cat-police procedure to have a search warrant in order to look round someone's premises? I have my privacy rights as a citizen-cat, don't I?"

Jack gestured to Marmaduke with his paw. "I think we may as well go, Cat-Constable Marmaduke. If Mr Splish is not prepared to cooperate with the cat-police, perhaps we'll have to make sure that he *does,* the next time we pay him a visit. Thank you for your time, Mr Splish."

Out in the Panda car Jack and Marmaduke sat without speaking for a few moments. It was Jack who broke the silence. "I wonder if he's got stolen merchandise in one of the rooms at the back of the building."

"Could be. And what a shabby place to run a business from."

"It wouldn't surprise me if his business was in trouble," said Jack. "That would be a pretty good motive for robbing Sir Lancelot's yacht. I think we should also check out the Kitty Kat Ice Cream Parlour. I wonder if they've had anything go missing."

The Same Day – Crime Room Meeting

All the cat-constables and cadet-cats of the Cat-Haven Cat-Police were gathered together in the Crime Room. Jack and Marmaduke had only just arrived in the office after their meeting with Willy Splish. They were all waiting for the 10.00 o'clock meeting that Stanley had called.

As he often did, Jumping Jack had jumped up onto his desk and was telling a few jokes.

"What's the difference between a cat and a comma?" he said with a grin on his face.

In contrast the faces of all the other cats were a complete blank. "No idea," said Tammy. "What's the answer Jack?" said Pamela excitedly.

"Well ....." said Jack slowly, "it's obvious really .... one has the paws before the claws .... and the other has the clause before the pause! Ha! Ha! Ha!"

All the cats bar one laughed, most especially

Soppy Cynthia, who exclaimed, "I got that one, Jack. It's a really good one!" She was beaming from ear to ear.

The exception was Studious Stephen. "Huh!" he said. "I didn't think it was that funny! And it certainly wasn't interesting. I'll tell you something that is interesting, Not many cats know this ..... a comma butterfly is an orange-brown butterfly, which has a white comma shaped mark on the underside of its wing."

There was complete silence in the Crime Room, until Marmaduke said, "that's reeally, reeeally, reeeeally interesting, Stephen!"

"OK, here's another one, especially for you, Cyn" said Jack. Soppy Cynthia's face lit up. "Knock, knock."

"Who's there?" replied Cynthia

"Boo!"

"Boo who?"

"Oh, I'm so sorry, Cyn, I didn't mean to make you cry! Ha! Ha! Ha!"

Cynthia's face was a picture of pure delight. She clapped her paws together with great enthusiasm. "You are awful, Jack. But I like you! Ha! Ha! Ha! How about another one?"

"OK," said Jack. "What did the police-cat say to his stomach?"

"Tell us, Jack," shouted out Pamela.

"Yes, tell us, Jack," echoed Cynthia.

"You're under a vest! Ha! Ha! Ha!"

There was so much laughter that no-one heard the Crime Room door open. Stanley and Derek came marching in. Derek looked furious.

Jack, however, was quick to try and take the heat out of the situation. "Hey, Sarge," he said, "your waistcoat and trousers are specdoinkel!"

In spite of himself Stanley smiled. He was wearing a new pair of trousers he had bought from NextKat over the weekend. They were sky blue with a profusion of purple spots. He had also bought a new waistcoat at the weekend, at Cats and Spencers. It was a pale, soft yellow, with on both sides the letters M E O W picked out vertically in blue. His bow tie had broad stripes of orange and matching sky blue.

Stanley raised his eyebrows at Jack. There was a warning look on his face. Jack jumped down from the top of his desk, grinning broadly. "Just passing the time, Sarge, while we were waiting for you and the Chief."

"You would be better off writing up your report on your visit to Splash Splosh Painters and Decorators," said Derek.

"Well ...." said Jack, "we've only been back a few minutes, Chief, and Marmaduke wanted to add another name to the Incident Board."

"That sounds promising, Jack," said Stanley.

Jack was pleased with himself. He thought he had quite neatly got out of any trouble over his joke telling.

"OK, settle down cats" said Derek in a loud voice. "We are going to have a meeting about the Harbour Murder." He looked over his shoulder at Stanley, who had followed him into the Crime Room. "Are we calling the case the Harbour Master-cat Murder, Stan?"

"Bit of a mouthful, isn't it? Perhaps it would be better, Chief, if we called it the Harbour Robbery and Murder Mysteries, since we've got a murder and a robbery on a yacht. They may well be linked, and I think we should review both incidents together for the time being. Let's have a look at the Incident Board."

"Let's keep it simple and just call the two cases The Harbour Mystery," said Derek.

"Well, it's better than a slap in the eye with a wet fish!" said Stanley. "Sorry, Chief, I didn't mean that. Actually, it's sooooo cool."

"It's specdoinkel!" said a grinning Jack.

Derek looked pleased with himself. "Ok cats, I'm going to hand over to Stanley to take us through what we know so far. Can you all please look at the Incident Board."

Cat-Haven Cat-Police

INCIDENT BOARD

CASE: 879 Murder of Bosun Brian, Harbourmaster-cat at Brixcat Harbour

CASE: 878 Theft from Flower of Catminster Yacht owned by Sir Lancelot

SUSPECTS & OTHERS

Last updated: 13th December

SUSPECTS - MURDER	INFORMATION TO HAND	MOTIVE
Bouncing Bert Assistant Harbourmaster-cat	Wants us to believe Brian tripped, which caused him to fall into the sea? Acts suspiciously. Lied about no cat staying with dead body.	? To get top job as Harbourmaster-cat
Mackerel Mike Fishercat	Fishes for mackerel from Brixcat Harbour. Has disappeared. Freddie surprised that he had come from the direction of the offices, not the fish unloading area.	No apparent motive
Fishercat Freddie Fishercat	Fishes for mackerel from Brixcat Harbour. He and Mackerel Mike pulled Bosun Brian out of the sea. Suggested Mike was "relieved" that Brian was dead	No apparent motive
Precious Gemma Brian's Wife	Works as sales assistant at Cat-Diamonds "R" Us. Has not acted like a grieving widow. Showed no emotion when she saw her husband's body. Hasn't been at work since the day after the murder.	Huge payout on Insurance Policy taken out recently on Brian's life.
Ship-Shape Shane Commodore-cat at Brixcat Yacht Club	Has key to Sir Lancelot's yacht. Knew about death very soon after it occurred.	No apparent motive

134

SUSPECTS - ROBBERY	INFORMATION	MOTIVE
Sir Lancelot Smiles-a-Lot	Politician-cat. One of his companies owns Flower of Catminster yacht. Cash and jewels stolen from safe in bedroom of yacht	Large Insurance Policy payable if jewels not found
Willy Splish Painter and Decorator	Owner of Splash Splosh Painters & Decorators. Last tradescat to have access to Sir L's yacht. Has not returned the key, although decorating job is finished.	His decorating business seems to be doing badly. ? has money problems
EVIDENCE - MURDER	**INFORMATION**	**COMMENTS**
Boathook	Found in sea at Brixcat Harbour. DNA evidence of blood and hairs of Bosun Brian. The letters FC-BH03 are on the handle. One perfect pawprint on handle	The Murder Weapon
Anchor	Rusty old anchor was attached to boathook to keep it on the sea bed	Suggests that the killer had knowledge of sea and access to anchor and boathook
EVIDENCE - ROBBERY		
Yale Key – silver in colour	Found in Master Bedroom on Sir L's yacht	
Pawprint	Found on painting in Master Bedroom on Sir L's yacht	Waiting analysis

The Same Day –
Crime Room Meeting

"Right," said Stanley, "let's consider what we know about Bouncing Bert. He's definitely acting suspiciously."

"I know what I think, Stan," said Derek. "I think he's guilty."

"Guilty of what, Chief?"

"Of the murder, of course."

"It's a bit soon to say that, Chief. We haven't got any evidence."

"I hear what you say, Stan, but I still think he's the guilty cat."

"He does seem to have tried to convince us that Bosun Brian tripped and fell, and hit his head on something. We now know that *that* isn't true."

"Excuse me, Sarge, but how do we know he didn't trip?" said Soppy Cynthia, a puzzled expression on her face.

Studious Stephen was quick to jump in. "Because we have the murder weapon, stupid!"

"That's enough Stephen," said Stanley. "We know he didn't trip, Cynthia," he said kindly, "because his blood and some of his hairs were found on the boathook, and he had a head injury which Annie told us was probably caused by something heavy. So it means that some cat struck him on the head with the boathook."

Cynthia was blushing furiously. "Thank you, Sarge. I see that now."

Stanley continued. "We also know that he lied when he said that he was surprised that neither Mackerel Mike nor Fishercat Freddie had stayed with the dead body. But Freddie told us that he *knew* that both he and Mike had to rush off, because they *told* him so."

"Could Freddie have been lying about that?" said Katie. This was her first contribution to a general meeting, and there was a nervous tremor in her voice.

"It's possible," said Stanley, "but I would think it was unlikely. Equally it's difficult to understand why Bert would have lied about something so unimportant."

"Perhaps he was just confused about who said what," said Jack. "I mean presumably he was in shock. After all, his boss was lying there dead."

"Good point, Jack." Stanley stroked his chin with his paw. "Bert does have a possible motive of course.

He now has the top job. What we need to establish is how important that fact is."

"Excuse me, Sarge." It was Cynthia again. She stood up and took her notebook out of her pocket. "When I was interviewing some of the cats who were in the office building, I made a note of something which might help with that point." She flicked through the pages until she came to the note she was looking for. "Yes, here it is," she said. "There was a cat called Eberneezer the Sneezer ...."

Jack and Marmaduke both laughed out loud.

"I know," said Cynthia, smiling, "it is quite a funny name. Actually it was a bit difficult to understand exactly what he was saying, 'cos he kept sneezing all the time! Anyway .... he asked me if the Harbour Master-cat had been murdered, and I said it was too early to say exactly how he had died." Cynthia turned in Jack's direction and smiled at him. "It was Jack who told me not to say anything about how he died, and I just made that up about it being too early to say." Cynthia was obviously proud of how she had coped with that particular question. After all, it was the first time she had ever interviewed any cats. "Anyway .... Eberneezer said, 'I'll bet it was Bouncing Bert' ...." Cynthia paused, screwing up her face and concentrating like mad. She was trying to imitate Eberneezer's accent ".... 'what done 'im in.' Those were his actual words, Sarge." Cynthia looked pleased with herself and sat down.

"Love your cockney accent, Cyn," said Jack. Cynthia smiled, licked her paw, and wiped it across her face.

"Did you ask him what reason he had for saying that?" enquired Stanley, although he already knew what Cynthia's answer would be.

"No Sarge, I didn't," said Cynthia. She looked embarrassed, because she knew that she should have asked him that question.

"Hmm. I think we'll have to find out exactly what this Eberneezer the Sneezer knows. You did well, Cynthia." Stanley smiled a smile full of encouragement, and Cynthia looked happy.

The Same Day – Crime Room Meeting

"Let's move on," said Stanley. "We have to find out what's happened to Mackerel Mike."

"Perhaps *he's* the guilty cat," said Derek. "Otherwise why would he have run off? Yes, that's it. He *must* be guilty."

"They can't all be guilty, Chief!" said Tammy, digging Pamela in the ribs.

"I hear what you say, Tammy. I'm not completely stupid." Derek frowned. "But it is suspicious, him running away like that."

There were a few giggles from some of the cats. This prompted Jack to jump up out of his chair and run over to the stationery cupboard, which was two metres high. He rocked back and forth on his paws, and then with a huge effort he leaped up into the air, and landed ever so softly on top of the cupboard.

"I think I know a joke about a cat who ran away from a mouse!" he said with a huge grin on his face.

"Not now, Jack," interrupted Stanley. Unusually for him, he was a bit angry. "For goodness sake stop clowning around and get down off that cupboard. We all know you can jump higher than any other cat in the Cat-Haven Cat Police, and we all hope you win the gold medal for the Cat High Jump at the Cat Olympics in London. But this is not the time for practising high jumps."

Derek joined in, his face reddening and his voice shaking. "You should know better, Jack. This is a serious discussion about a serious c-c-c-c-c- crime. It's not the time for telling jokes, any sort of jokes; old jokes, good jokes, corny jokes, rib-tickling jokes, side splitting jokes, even f-f-f-f-f-funny jokes." Derek was now purple in the face and many of the cats in the Crime Room were either laughing, or trying not to laugh! Jack jumped down from the cupboard and went back to his chair. As he passed Marmaduke he gave him a huge wink, which he knew that neither Derek nor Stanley could see.

"We do need to discover where Mackerel Mike is," said Stanley, taking over. "Jack, I want you and Marmaduke to go round to his house and talk to some of his neighbours. Let's establish whether or not he's run away."

"Perhaps he's just on holiday," said Katie. "That would be a simple answer."

"I agree," said Pamela, only because she thought she ought to say something.

"What do you think, Vincent?" said Marmaduke mischievously.

Vincent was staring out of the window, completely unaware that anyone had spoken to him.

"Vincent?" repeated Marmaduke.

Vincent suddenly stood up, ignoring Marmaduke. "Sorry, Sarge," he said with a troubled expression on his face. "I need to go for a poo!"

"Typical," said Jack.

"Go on then," said Stanley, trying not to sound angry. Vincent literally ran from the office, his paw clutching his bum. His black face was screwed up in agony. He shot through the office door like an arrow from a bow! Most of the cats in the room were laughing. Tammy had thrown herself on the ground, and lay on her back. Pamela was quick to join her on the floor and tickle Tammy's tummy. Soppy Cynthia also threw herself on the ground, and tried to tickle her own tummy. Marmaduke shouted, "go Vinnny go .... go Vinny go .... go Vinny go." Jack clapped his paws together. Only Studious Stephen failed to join in the fun. He picked up his latest book, *Cod Fishing in the North Cat-Sea*, riffled through a few pages, and then started to read.

"You sure you're in the right place, Stephen?" said Jack.

"Am I herring you right, Jack?" said Marmaduke.

"Cod you have said plaice? Did you like that, Jack?"

"What, you fishing for a compliment, Marmy?"

Chief Inspector Derek Dimwit was beside himself with rage. "This isn't g-g-g-g-g good enough. I'm f-f-f-f-f-furious with all of you. I'm going to c-c-c-c-c-c-cancel lunch ...... except for Stanley and me of course."

Tammy jumped up off the floor, and was about to open her mouth to complain, until she saw Marmaduke shake his head in a not now gesture. She realised that it would be better to let the storm blow over.

"For goodness sake," said Stanley once more, "let's get back to the matter in hand. "Does anyone have any comments to make about Fishercat Freddie?" Stanley's question was greeted in silence. "I don't think there's anything to suggest he had anything to do with either crime," he went on. "So let's move on to Precious Gemma. She certainly doesn't seem to have been very upset about her husband's death."

Derek Dimwit was about to say something, but changed his mind at the last moment. He seemed to have calmed down a bit.

"Apparently she hasn't been at work since last Thursday," said Stanley. "In view of the fact that she stands to benefit from his death, by getting a substantial amount of money, we need to interview her. She's obviously got a strong motive for wanting her husband dead."

The Same Day –
Crime Room Meeting

"Jack, would you like to give us your impressions of Ship-Shape Shane, please."

"Yes, Sarge," responded Jack. "Both me and Marmaduke thought he was a bit of a strange cat, and he was pretty disorganised. He didn't seem to keep very good records. And he wasn't very helpful. We had to squeeze answers to our questions out of him. The only thing that at the time we thought was of interest was that he knew that the Harbour Master-cat was dead. We wondered how he could have known. But we checked it out with Nosey Nathan, and he confirmed that he had told Shane, after he learned it from the Chief. Was there anything else, Marmy?"

"The only thing I would add is that we thought he doesn't get on very well with Sir Lancelot," said Marmaduke. "We got the impression that he doesn't like him."

Stanley smiled. "Can't say I blame him for that. We didn't like Sir Lancelot very much either, did we Chief?"

Derek nodded, but said nothing.

"We do know that Sir Lancelot, or rather his company, has the jewels well insured, so he won't be out of pocket as a result of the theft. We have no reason to suppose that he was responsible for the theft, but we should at least not rule him out at this stage."

"I did have another thought about Sir Lancelot," said Jack. "You know there's been such a lot of publicity about members of the cat-parliament fiddling their expenses. Well, presumably they can't take the risk of trying to do that anymore. So that might mean that some of them are going to be short of money. They'll have to find other ways of getting money to carry on with their luxury lifestyles! Maybe that's the situation with Sir Lancelot?"

"Interesting thought, Jack." Stanley paused for a moment. "Tammy," he then said, "I'd like you to see what you can find out about Sir Lancelot's financial affairs."

Tammy was thrilled. "Of course I will, Sarge," she replied.

"If he's short of money, that would certainly give him a motive for stealing his own jewels."

The Same Day – Crime Room Meeting

"Marmaduke," said Stanley, "please tell us about your visit this morning to the decorating business Splash Splosh."

"Well, Sarge, me and Jack went to their offices this morning and interviewed a cat called Willy Splish. He decorated the main lounge bar area on the yacht about a month ago, and claimed that he didn't go into the master bedroom. The reason he kept the key is that it's his policy to hold on to keys till the customer has paid. And he said Sir Lancelot hasn't paid him. He called it an 'insurance policy'. With a bit of persuasion we got him to tell us that he also has the key to the Kitty Kat Ice Cream Parlour. He said they hadn't paid his bill either. Apparently there was a dispute about the quality of his work."

"His office was pretty skanky, wasn't it, Jack?"

"Yeah! It was pants! Considering he's a painter and

decorator it was a joke. His office is desperately in need of some fresh paint! Generally speaking, Sarge," Jack continued, "he was uncooperative. At the end of the interview we asked him if we could have a look round his premises. He refused. Told us we needed a search warrant. It suggested to us that he might have something to hide."

"Agreed," said Stanley, nodding his head.

"One other thing. His front door was really battered. It looked like he had had a break in. And two new locks had been fitted. Pretty recently, we thought."

"Was one of the new locks a Yale lock?"

"Yes!" said Jack and Marmaduke at the same time. They grinned at each other.

"Very interesting," said Stanley.

The Same Day –
Crime Room Meeting

Stanley rested his chin on one paw, and with the other furiously scratched the underside of his chin. "OK," he said after a few moments of thought, and scratching, "we'll come back to Willy Splish shortly. For the moment, let's discuss the boathook. Thanks to Annie we know that it was definitely the murder weapon. Has anyone got any ideas on what **FCBH03** might mean?"

Katie looked round in case one of the other cats was going to speak, but none of them did. She decided to contribute her thoughts. "I did have one idea, Sarge," she said. "Do you think **FC** might be the initials of Sir Lancelot's yacht, Flower of Catminster? And **BH03** may simply stand for boathook number three?"

Stanley gazed at Katie with his unblinking blue eyes for a few moments. "I think that's an inspired guess, Katie. When you and Pamela go over to Brixcat Harbour with the photographs of the boathook and the anchor, you could start with checking out the boathooks on the yacht. If your guess is right there will probably be other similar boathooks on board. While you're there I'd like you to interview Eberneezer the Sneezer and find out why he was so quick to blame Bouncing Bert for the murder of the Harbour Master-cat." Stanley paused to lick his fur, which gave Jack the opportunity to jump in.

"When you go there Sis," he said, winking at Katie, "make sure to take plenty of tissues with you. In case he sneezes all over you!" Cynthia laughed like a drain.

"Jack," said Stanley, "I'd like you and Marmaduke to take the Yale key and visit the Splash Splosh premises tomorrow, outside office hours, and see whether it fits the lock on the front door."

"If it does fit," said Jack, "shall we go in and have a nose around?"

Stanley thought about this for a bit, and then said, "No, I don't think so, Jack. If we do decide that we want to have a look round we'll go down the proper route and get a search warrant."

The Next Day – Tuesday 13th December

Sir Lancelot Smiles-a-Lot stepped out of a shocking pink Kool 4 Kats Taxi outside the offices of the Cat-Haven Chronicle. He was wearing an expensive grey and black pin-stripe suit. The heavy, early morning rain had stopped, but there were puddles on the pavement. A blue eyed, snow white kitten, wearing bright green wellington boots, was riding past on a tricycle. His mother shouted at him "Don't ride through that puddle, Corky!" Naturally Corky pretended not to hear, and veered at an angle so that he could ride straight through the centre of the puddle. Spray shot up, and covered Sir Lancelot's shiny black leather shoes. Corky's mother found it difficult not to laugh. Corky rode on, unaware of Sir Lancelot's rage. "I'm sorry, Sir," said Corky's mother.

"So you should be," replied Sir Lancelot

unpleasantly. "Why can't you keep your brat under control!"

Corky's mother raised her paw to her nose and waggled her claws in a gesture of defiance. "Lighten up, you old fool. Can't you see, my kitten's just having fun."

Sir Lancelot glowered at the mother-cat and swept into the revolving doors that led into the newspaper's offices. He took a final murderous glance at Corky and his mother. Unfortunately, his anger clouded his judgement of distance. Instead of waiting patiently for the opening of the revolving door, he rushed ahead, slipping on the wet ground. He slithered straight into the moving glass, cracked his head, and fell to the ground in a heap. Simile Emily, the receptionist-cat, who was sitting at a huge semi circular desk, burst out laughing. Sir Lancelot scowled in her direction, and struggled to his feet. Rubbing his head, he marched up to the desk and demanded. "I want to see your editor-cat."

Emily whispered to herself, "and now your smile's as bright as the night!"

"What did you say?" said Sir Lancelot agressively.

"Nothing." She shook her head from side to side. "Do you have an appointment?"

"If I had an appointment I would have said so."

"No need to be as unpleasant as a stinky pheasant," said Simile Emily, who just couldn't help using similes whenever she had the chance. She was hoping that one day she would get the opportunity to be a reporter, and write stories for the newspaper. It was a sort of practice for her. "Who are you anyway?"

"Don't you know who I am?"

"No, should I?" Emily was giving as good as she got.

"I'm Sir Lancelot Smiles-a-Lot. I'm a member of the Cat-Parliament in Catminster, and I have a humungous, luxury yacht moored in Brixcat Harbour. It's about my yacht that I want to see the editor-cat. What's his name?"

"Poisonous Paddy the Pen," replied Emily. "I'll see if he's available." She picked up the phone and dialled an internal number. "Hello PP, I've got an awful cat out here. He's as unpleasant as a skanky pheasant, as angry as a bear with a sore head, and as ugly as a pig with his snout plastered with mud. He says he wants to see the editor-cat." As she listened to Paddy's words she stared directly at Sir Lancelot, her green eyes unblinking. She held the phone away from her mouth, and said to him in a voice full of derision. "Who are you again?"

Sir Lancelot was beside himself with anger. "How dare you be so disrespectful! I've told you once already, you stupid cat. I'm Sir Lancelot Smiles-a-Lot!"

"Oh yes," said Emily, speaking into the phone once more, "he's that dreadful politician-cat with the smiling teeth. I've heard that his promises last as long as it takes for a cup of water to reach the ground when it's been turned upside down." An audible chuckle could be heard from the other end of the phone. "You don't really want to see him, do you?" she said picking her teeth with an open claw. Another chuckle was followed by a pause, and then she very carefully put the phone down. "Take a seat over there," she said to Sir Lancelot, pointing to a row of chairs. "The editor-cat will grant you a short interview, probably as short as your plastic smile usually lasts! You'll have to wait until he's available."

Fully five minutes later, Poisonous Paddy strolled into the reception area. He was a tall, slim cat, an American Burmese breed, with gorgeous deep brown fur and rounded golden eyes. He was casually dressed in an open necked blue shirt, blue jeans and expensive trainers. A superior smile hovered on his lips. "What can I do for you Sir Lancelot?"

"I want you to run an article in your newspaper about the jewellery stolen from my yacht."

"Are you offering a reward?" said Paddy

"Certainly not," said Sir Lancelot.

"What's the news angle?"

"There isn't an angle!" Sir Lancelot went red in the face. "It's a disgrace, that's what it is. My yacht was parked in Brixcat Harbour. I'm a very important cat. You should know that."

"I think it's a job for the Cat-Police," said Paddy, "not a newspaper."

"Can't you do something? Appeal to the thief to give me back my jewels? Ask your readers for information?"

"There's a murder investigation going on, Sir

Lancelot. That seems to me to be a rather more important story."

"There's nothing more important than the robbery on board my yacht, and I think you should treat it seriously!"

"We'll give it the consideration it deserves," sniffed Poisonous Paddy.

"I don't think you realise who you're dealing with. If you don't bring this matter to the attention of the cat-public, I'll make it my business to see that you're punished."

A mischievous smile settled on Poisonous Paddy's lips, and he cocked his head to one side. "This interview is over," he said with finality. With that he turned his back on Sir Lancelot, swished his tail, and strode out of the reception area.

Sir Lancelot was not used to being dismissed and his cheeks almost burst at the seams. He had never been so angry. Emily, who had witnessed the entire conversation, grinned stupidly.

"You had better watch your step, too," snarled Sir Lancelot. "I'll have you sacked for insolence if I choose to." He did his best to recover his composure, and stalked out of the Cat-Haven Chronicle offices.

As he left the building, Emily rubbed her paws together in anticipation. She couldn't wait to see what Poisonous Paddy's response would be to the arrogant Sir Lancelot Smiles-a-Lot. It should make enjoyable reading!

The Same Day

P amela and Katie were travelling in a blue Panda car, which they had taken from the car park at the cat-police station. They were on their way to Brixcat Harbour to interview Eberneezer the Sneezer. They were also going to check out the boathook, which was now established as the murder weapon.

"How are you settling in to the new job, Katie?" asked Pamela.

"I think I'm really going to like it," said Katie. "Everyone's been so nice to me."

"How are you coping with not being able to skate now?"

"It's difficult, obviously. I do miss it. But that's life. You can't have everything you want. And of course, whatever problem or difficulty *you* have, there are always some cats who are worse off. You have to make the best of what life gives you."

"I think you'll enjoy this afternoon. It should be

fun. According to Marmy, in order to get out to the yacht, we have to use a small rowing boat!"

As they pulled in to the harbour entrance Pamela said, "I think we'll see if we can interview Eberneezer the Sneezer first. By the way, did you bring plenty of tissues?"

Katie laughed. "Yes, I've got a whole pack of Kleenex-cat! Pity one of us wasn't a nurse, then we could have brought face masks!"

Nosey Nathan, the security-cat, was out of his booth in a flash. He was about to tell them where to park when he realised that the driver was none other than the love of his life. As Pamela and Katie walked towards him, a large lump of yellow-green snot dripped from his nose onto his clean, white, security-cat shirt. Immediately he removed it with his paw and threw it onto the ground.

"Oh, that's revolting," said Pamela, turning her head away.

Nathan was struck dumb. How could that possibly have happened to me in front of my special cat friend? If I'd known it was her, I'd have made sure to blow my nose before stepping out of the booth. He didn't even know her name, and had been going to ask her. But not now of course.

"Good morning cat-constable," he managed to say.

Pamela shook her head in disgust. "My cat-police colleague and I want to see Eberneezer the Sneezer."

Her face was unsmiling, her manner cold.

"I'll buzz up to him," Nathan replied. "If you could just wait a moment." He retraced his steps, returned to his booth, and picked up the phone. While he was waiting for someone to answer he picked his nose, examined what was on the end of his claw, and put it in his mouth.

"Yuck!" said Pamela and Katie at the same moment. They turned their heads away, feeling slightly sick.

"That is one horrendous cat!" said Pamela.

"With one horrendous conk!" exclaimed Katie, trying to lighten the mood. "I've never seen such an awful nose. It looks like a squashed tomato!"

Pamela burst out laughing. At that moment Nathan attempted to step out from the booth. He tripped on the telephone flex and disappeared from view. "He always does that," said Pamela.

Nathan picked himself up and was just in time to hear Katie say, "I guess his nose is so big it stops him from seeing his feet."

Pamela guffawed once more. "I reckon it looks more like two squashed tomatoes jammed together. With two holes at one end!"

Katie and Pamela couldn't stop laughing. "If he was a horse, I bet he'd feed from a nosebag," said Katie.

Then it was Pamela's turn. "And if he was a racehorse he'd probably win all his races by a nose!"

"Don't say that," said Katie. "You'll put his nose out of joint!"

The two female cats clutched their ribs and bent double with laughter.

Nathan momentarily closed his eyes, and wished that the ground under his paws would open up and swallow him. But no such luck. "Have you finished?" he said sadly. "Eberneezer the Sneezer is expecting you. Turn left at the top of the steps. It's the third door on the right."

As the two cat-police climbed the stone steps up to the building's first floor, Katie whispered. "A lot of cats round here seem to have a nose problem."

Eberneezer the Sneezer was a black cat with white socks. Mercifully he seemed to be in the middle of a rest period in terms of sneezing.

Pamela made the introductions, and both she and Katie showed Eberneezer their warrant cards. "We understand," she started, "that you told one of our colleagues last Wednesday that you thought Bosun Brian had been murdered by Bouncing Bert. Why was that?"

"I didn't exactly say that," said Eberneezer. "I said it wouldn't surprise me if he was the cat what dunnit. Not quite the same thing."

"What made you think it was possible?"

"It was well known that Bert and Brian didn't get along. In fact they didn't like each other. Bert was always complainin' that Brian was a pants Harbour Master-cat. He didn't rate him as the bosun of the lifeboat either. I had to go out on the lifeboat once when Brian wasn't available. Bert took over as the bosun, and he didn't stop slaggin' Brian off. When the job of the Harbour Master-cat came up, they both went for it. Bert was very bitter that he lost. He had been workin' at the harbour longer than Brian. In fact he was already the assistant Harbour Master-cat, and everyone thought that he would automatically get the top job."

"Why didn't he?" asked Katie.

"Nobody really knew. There were whispers."

"What sort of whispers?" said Pamela.

"There was no proof, you understand, but some cats thought that Brian must have bribed the Mayor. To be honest, it was Bert who was spreadin' the rumour."

"How long ago was all this?" asked Pamela.

"Not all that long. About nine months, that's all."

Pamela continued. "Why did the job come up?"

"The previous Harbour Master-cat retired."

"Did Bert ever make any threats against Brian?" asked Katie.

Eberneezer paused. He started to wrinkle up his nose and his eyes became moist. His shoulders shook and his whole body became tense. It seemed like he was about to sneeze!

"A-a-a-a-a!" Katie and Pamela each took a step back. Katie withdrew a tissue from her pocket.

"A-a-a-a-a!" Katie and Pamela looked on. Nervously! "A-a-a-a-a! A-a-a-a-a-a.... tish.....

ooooooooooo! When finally the sneeze came it was more like a thunderclap than a sneeze. A spray of fine liquid bubbles shot out of Eberneezer's nostrils. He made a serious effort to point his nose downwards so that the spray from his nose would not go over Pamela and Katie. Fortunately for them, and unfortunately for him, what came out of his nose drenched his own shirt. He wiped his paw over it. There was a look of pure disgust on Pamela's face. "Unbelievable!" she said quietly as she turned away.

"So... so sorry about that," said Eberneezer. "It's a medical problem I've got. I just can't help it!"

"So ....." continued Katie, trying to hide her embarrassment, "did Bert make any threats against Brian?"

"Well ...." said Eberneezer, regaining his composure, "I can't really say. I didn't hear anythin' myself. But accordin' to Mackerel Mike they had a huge bust up a week or so ago. They came to blows."

"Do you know why?"

"No, sorry."

Katie made a note in her notebook. "When did Mackerel Mike tell you this?"

Eberneezer scratched his chin. "I think it was the day before Brian died. I bumped into him in Brixcat Tea Rooms. He said he'd been talkin' to Bert that mornin' after he got back from fishin'. Bert was really angry about Brian punchin' him in the face a couple of days earlier. And he had a huge bruise and a black eye to show for it. Mike asked him what they had argued about, but Bert wouldn't tell him. The only thing he did say was that if Brian ever did that to him again he would kill him."

"Thank you, Eberneezer," said Katie. "You've been most helpful." She made a few more notes in her notebook.

"One other thing," said Pamela pulling two photographs out of her pocket. "Have you seen either a boathook or an anchor like these?"

Eberneezer studied the photographs and then shook his head. "I'm afraid not."

As Pamela and Katie closed the office door behind them, they heard a sound like an exploding bomb, and the door handle in Katie's paw shook violently. It was Eberneezer. Sneezing!

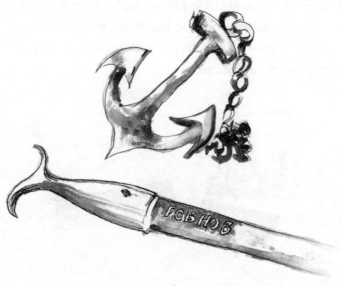

The Same Day

S hip-Shape Shane looked up from his desk as Pamela and Katie entered the Cat-Haven Yacht Club. "What can I do for you?" he said.

Pamela made the introductions. "I'm Cat-Constable Playful Pamela, and this is my colleague-cat Cadet-Cat Skatie Katie. We're following up on the robbery on Sir Lancelot's yacht. First of all," she went on, "could you please look at these photographs. Can you tell us if you recognise either the boathook or the anchor?"

Katie pulled the photos out of her pocket and pawed them to Shane.

Shane studied the two photos carefully. "No," he said at length. "I haven't seen either of them before. They look pretty ordinary to me. They could be off any boat. Anyway what have they got to do with the robbery?"

Pamela didn't respond to Shane's question. "Well, thank you anyway, Shane. The main reason we're here is to arrange to go out to the Flower of Catminster yacht."

Shane's craggy face crumpled into a false smile. He scratched his scruffy beard. "Are you sure? I assume you know that you have to row a boat out to the yacht?"

"We were hoping some kind cat could row us out there," said Katie.

"When did you want to go?"

"Now .... if it's possible." Katie did her best to smile sweetly.

"How long would you expect to be on the yacht?"

"Not long. About ten or fifteen minutes." Katie looked at Pamela for confirmation. Pamela nodded.

"Hmm! I suppose I could row you out there."

"That would be so kind of you," gushed Pamela. "We really would be grateful."

Twenty minutes later the three cats were climbing aboard the Flower of Catminster.

"What exactly are you looking for?" asked Shane as they made their way into the main cabin.

Katie was about to open her mouth, but she saw Pamela's warning look.

"Just carrying out basic cat-police procedures. You don't have to follow us around, Shane," said Pamela rather pointedly.

"I suppose you want to examine the safe."

Pamela looked at Shane thoughtfully. "Thank you, Shane. We'll call you when we're ready to leave." With that, Pamela, with Katie hard on her heels, turned her back on Shane and left the main cabin.

"Do you know where this leads to?" whispered Katie.

Pamela smiled. "Yes, Jack gave me an idea of the layout of the deck. We should come to the bedroom at the end of this corridor."

"I thought we wanted to check out the boathook?"

"We do, but I wanted to get rid of Shane. We don't want him breathing down our necks while we're here. And anyway I don't trust him."

"I agree with you about that," said Katie. "He seems a bit slippery."

"Oh yes, and I hate cats with beards!"

Katie laughed. "And it makes it horrible to kiss them!"

"Yuck," exclaimed Pamela. "You don't want to kiss Shane do you?"

They both laughed.

They spent a couple of minutes examining the master bedroom for any clues that Jack and Marmaduke might have missed. They found nothing.

However, as they were leaving the cabin a strong breeze flapped at the curtain covering an open porthole. It riffled the pages of a newspaper that was lying on the floor, next to the framed painting of the Golden Hindcat. It dislodged a scrap of white paper.

"Where did that come from?" said Katie, picking it up. Its edges were jagged, and it seemed to have been torn from a larger piece of paper.

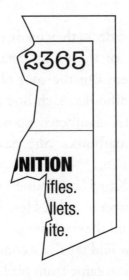

Katie passed the piece of paper to Pamela. "What do you make of that?"

"Curious," said Pamela. "Who knows? It looks like it's been torn from something. Perhaps it's just a corner of some piece of paper. We'll take it back to the office. It might be significant."

The Same Day

Back up on deck, they made their way towards the bow of the yacht. Shane was nowhere to be seen. On the roof of the front cabin was a pair of boathooks, each one clipped into two metal cleats. Katie clambered up onto the roof and unclipped the boathooks. She passed them down to Pamela.

"Clever little Katie!" said Pamela with a broad grin on her face. "You were right. Here it is ... **FCBH04** and **FCBH07**. And they've both got the same cut-out for a cat's paw. I would say that's conclusive proof that the murder weapon came from Sir Lancelot's yacht."

"Let's check for the anchor too," said Katie clambering down back onto the deck.

"Where are anchors normally kept, do you know, Katie?"

"Not really. I guess they're either stored somewhere at the front of the boat, or perhaps at the back."

Pamela laughed. "I take it you're not really a boat

cat then! I think they call it the bow and the stern, don't they?"

Katie laughed too. "I'm sure you're right."

The only thing they could find attached to the deck at the bow end of the Yacht was a heavy metal chain, about a metre in length. The very last link at the end of the chain was almost twice the size of the other links. "Do you think the anchor is normally kept at the end of this chain? Attached to the larger link at the end?"

Pamela shrugged her shoulders. "Could be," she said. "In fact, thinking about it, it makes sense."

They searched the rest of the yacht, including the entire deck area at the stern, but could not find an anchor, or any other evidence of where one might be kept.

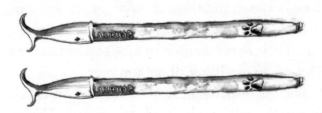

The Same Day

"How do I look, Jackster?" said Marmaduke with a huge smile on his face. His claws were covered with solid gold rings, he had a simple gold necklace round his neck, and a boat-shaped earring in each ear.

"Specdoinkel!" replied Jack. "All blinged up and ready to go!" He too wore a gold ring on every one of his eight claws, and three chunky gold chains around his neck. His gold earrings were like miniature golf balls. They were standing in Jack's apartment, ready to set off to the Bling Bling Bar.

They had spent most of the afternoon checking out the flat where Mackerel Mike lived. There was no sign of him. According to various neighbours he hadn't been seen for several days, although as more than one cat pointed out, this meant little. In the winter months most cats kept to themselves, and you could go weeks without seeing your next door neighbour. Asking around, it seemed that he was a frequent visitor to the Bling Bling Bar. Jack and Marmaduke had decided to visit the bar to see what they could find out.

They left Jack's apartment shortly after seven o'clock and drove into the centre of town. They parked in the multi storey car park, and walked round the corner towards the station. They strolled over the level crossing, and on down Torcat Road. The Bling Bling Bar was next to a fish and chip shop, two doors away from the Chop Suey-Cat Chinese restaurant, and had gaudy red neon lettering announcing its name. And there was an illuminated sign, again in red, which flashed on and off, and announced:

'EVERY CAT'S DELIGHT – CHEAP BEER EVERY NIGHT'

As usual the bar was guarded by two huge, heavyweight bouncer-cats wearing white waistcoats. They were there to enforce the bar's unusual, but strict, entry rules. Every cat who wanted to enter had to be wearing a large amount of bling, preferably gold. There were no exceptions. Jack and Marmaduke were 'properly dressed' and were waved in.

Within moments of entering the darkened bar Jack and Marmaduke heard a loud scream. It was a scream of delight, and it came from the lips of the waitress-cat behind the bar counter. She was Vodka Valentina, a stunningly pretty Russian Blue, tall and slim, with a coat of bright blue fur, tipped with a silvery sheen. Her vivid, electric green eyes shone with pleasure. "Mar.... meeeee," she shouted enthusiastically. She rushed from behind the bar and ran up to Marmaduke, throwing her paws round his neck and kissing him on both cheeks. "I didn't think I would see you till Friday!"

"You two got a date on Friday?" queried Jack, a mischievous twinkle dancing in his eyes, a broad grin on his face.

Marmaduke reddened slightly. "As a matter of fact we do, Jackster. As you already know!"

"Hello, Jack," said Valentina, "It's nice to seeing you."

She offered him her cheek, and he kissed it with warmth on his lips. "It's nice to see you too Valentina. I feel I know you better than my own sister – Marmy talks about you all the time!"

It was Valentina's turn to blush. "What would you like to drinking, both of you?"

"Orange juice please," said Jack and Marmaduke at almost the same time.

Valentina returned to her side of the bar and selected two tumblers from one of the shelves. "When I've poured your drinks, I'll go and make you some toast and marmalade," she said smiling at Marmaduke.

Hardly had Marmaduke thanked Valentina than a large Russian Blue came charging over to the bar. "Mar...mee!" he shouted. It was the Russian ice skating champion, Yuri Katakov, who for a long time, under the name of Beastly Boris, had been the prime suspect in the Mackerel Robberies case. On a previous visit to the Bling Bling Bar during that case, Marmaduke had stepped in when an ugly ginger tom had threatened Valentina. His bravery had earned him a bloody nose from the ginger tom, and the lifelong friendship of Yuri Katakov, who it turned out, was the brother of Valentina. Yuri almost crushed Marmaduke's ribs as he grasped him in a serious bear hug, and then planted noisy kisses on his cheeks. "How are you, my now and forever friend? Come, we drink some vodka together, no?"

"Unfortunately we can't, Yuri," responded Marmaduke. "We're on duty."

"Hello, Yuri," said Jack, "Good to see you. You might be able to help us."

"Anything I can do, I do," replied Yuri. "It is good to seeing you again, Jack, also."

"Do you know a fishercat called Mackerel Mike?"

Yuri's face clouded over. "Huh!" he said. "This cat, he tried steal my tuna sandwich! He no good cat."

"What happened?" said Marmaduke.

"He come in here many times this Mackerel Mike. He pretend to be friend. In fact I think he sweet on Valentina." Marmaduke's Seville orange complexion turned a deeper shade of red. Yuri patted him on the shoulder. "Don't worry, my now and forever friend, I tell Valentina he no good cat, and anyway she no like him neither. She only like you, Marmee. I had order tuna sandwich from Valentina. When she made it, she put it on bar counter. This Mackerel Mike he try to steal it and eat it. But my friend Sergei, he see what happen, and he smack this Mike hard in the mouth!" Yuri chuckled at the memory. "He no can eat tuna with swollen mouth!"

"When was the last time you saw him?" asked Marmaduke.

Yuri furiously scratched the back of his neck with his paw, just behind his ear. "Let me think ...." he said, continuing to scratch. ".... I guess was about five or six days ago. Valentina, she tell me later, that when he order drink from her he said he go to Tenerife on holiday."

"Did he tell her when he was going?" asked Jack.

"Not exact day, but he said it was soon. He said he go for one week."

"Perhaps that's where he is now, Jack," said Marmaduke. "On holiday."

"Could well be," replied Jack, nodding his head.

"Come, you join us at our table," insisted Yuri, taking Marmaduke by the paw. My friends they would like seeing you again, and say hello."

"Well, ok, just for a few minutes while I eat my toast and marmalade."

"Ah," said Yuri, winking furiously at Jack. "I guessing Valentina she make for you, no?" Yuri turned towards Jack. "You know, Jack my friend, we Russian cats, we have wise proverb. It go like this .... Female cat, she know way to winning heart of male cat, is to stuffing his gut with plenty his favourite food!" Yuri guffawed, and nudged Jack in the ribs. Jack laughed and Marmaduke went red once more!

"That reminds me of a joke," said Jack. "Why didn't the skeleton cross the road?"

Both Marmaduke and Yuri looked blank. "You tell us, Jack," said Yuri.

"It's obvious really. Because he didn't have the guts! Ha! Ha! Ha!"

Yuri clapped his head between his paws. "Hee, hee, hee, Jack! You tell the good jokes!"

The Same Day

Thick, heavy snow was falling when Jack and Marmaduke left the Bling Bling Bar and walked swiftly along Torcat Road towards the level crossing. Although it had been snowing for less than an hour, it was already settling on the pavements. The air was crisp and cold, and a full moon shone down on the already white roofs and chimneys of Cat-Haven-on-Sea. A silvery sheen seemed to tinge the buildings on the other side of the street. The cold had a bitter edge to it. It was the sort of cold that would chill the bones of even the sturdiest cat.

"Huh!" exclaimed Jack, buttoning up his overcoat. "All blinged up and snowhere to go!"

"Good one, Jackster," laughed Marmaduke.

Jack looked at his watch. It was nearly nine o'clock. "Have we got time to check out the Splash Splosh offices to see if that key fits?"

"Just about," replied Marmaduke. "We need to get a move on though. The snow seems to be setting

174

in for the night. The roads are sure to be icy soon. Come on, let's move."

Jack drove the panda car out of the multi-storey car park, which was situated on the other side of the level crossing. The thick snow continued to fall, and the car windscreen wipers were batting it from side to side in great chunks. "If this gets much worse we'll end up abandoning the car," said Jack with a grin.

When they reached Decorators Lane, they parked right outside the offices of Splash Splosh. They both got out of the car and approached the office door, leaving pawprints on the smooth snow surface of the pavement.

Jack took the key out of his pocket and placed it in the lock. "Bingo!" he said, as the key turned. "It's tempting to go in, Marmy. But I suppose we ought to leave it at that, as the Sarge suggested."

"Agreed," said Marmaduke.

They retraced their steps back to the car, leaving a fresh set of pawprints. They drove back to the cat-police car park, with the snow still falling heavily.

"At least we know the answer to one question," said Jack.

"Possibly two," replied Marmaduke. "We'll have to check with Thomas-cat Holidays tomorrow, and see whether they have any information on Mackerel Mike."

The Next Day –
Wednesday 14th December

Stanley was up early. He climbed out of bed and put on a white towelling dressing gown over his orange and green striped jimjams. It had been freezingly cold overnight and his central heating system was struggling to keep the house warm. He lived in a picturesque cottage, only a catapult's throw from Cat-Haven harbour. It had magnificent views of the great variety of boats moored in the harbour, and of the vastness of the sea. Not that he could see very much of the sea this morning, as he looked out of his kitchen window. A blanket of snow covered the ground, and dusted the boats in the harbour. It was a Christmas card scene. And Stanley realised he hadn't even bought any Christmas cards, let alone sent them. Not quite true, he thought. He had sent a couple of cards to America to his cousin Chuck and to Francesca Forensicca in California. Francesca had been Apple Pie Annie's predecessor, but homesickness had driven her back to the USA.

Usually, Stanley had freshly squeezed orange juice for breakfast. It always reminded him of James Bondcat. When he had made the mistake of telling this to Jack he had got a typical reply from one of his favourite police-cats. "I suppose that makes you 00 three and a half, Sarge, licensed to carry pawcuffs!" Stanley smiled at the memory. He decided he would go out for breakfast this morning.

After a hot shower, he dressed warmly. He chose a pair of trousers that he had recently bought from the upmarket clothing shop in town, Cats and Spencers. They were a dark red with squintillions of purple spots, and made of a warm fleecy material, ideal for a bone-chilling day. As usual he wore a bow tie and a waistcoat. His bow tie was a warm orange in colour with bright green spots, and his unusual waistcoat was dual coloured, with one panel of yellow and another of turquoise blue .

He stepped out of his cottage, wearing black, ankle length, fur boots and a serious overcoat. On his head he wore a genuine Russian fur hat, which had been given to him by Yuri Katakov. As he closed his front door he saw his next door neighbour, Colourful Christine, coming out of her house. She always wore really colourful clothes and despite the winter chill she still looked great. She had a spangly turquoise coat, bright red trousers and a pink roll neck sweater, although she could not see any of her clothes. Sadly she was a blind cat and carried a white stick. She was accompanied by a large, friendly looking German Shepherd.

"Morning, Christine," Stanley shouted across the three foot high hedge that separated the two cottages. "Is that a new Guide Dog you've got?"

"Yes he is, Stan. He's called Steve." She stroked the back of his head. "Steve," she said, "this is my neighbour, Stanley."

"Hello, mate," said Steve. "How you doing?"

"That is sooooo cool," said Stanley. "A dog that speaks cat-lingo! You must be very proud of him, Christine."

Steve barked softly. "Gruff gruff." It was more like clearing his throat than barking, a sort of low growl. "Of course she's proud of me, Stan, gruff gruff," he said, grinning. Round his neck he had a silver chain with a piece of snooker-type blue chalk hanging from it.

"Why the blue chalk on a chain, Steve?" asked Stanley.

"I used to be the World Snooker Champion. The way I used to play reminded everyone of Steve Davis-Cat, that's why they called me Steve, gruff gruff. I was world champion seven times, one more than Steve Davis-Cat. As a matter of fact, gruff gruff, I played him in a charity event a couple of weeks ago.

Best of five frames. Although I hadn't played for quite a while, I beat him easily. I made a few deliberate mistakes so he wouldn't be humiliated in front of the paying cats. So it was only three two. In the deciding frame I gave him a start leaving a few easy reds so he could get a bit of a score. In the end I snookered him on the pink, and he missed it. That gave me the game. I don't mind telling you, he was furious. Can't blame him really, gruff gruff – I think he was embarrassed to be beaten by a dog!" Steve wagged his tail furiously, but rather than from side to side he wagged it up and down.

"So when did you become a Guide dog?"

"After I retired from snooker I wanted a challenge really, gruff gruff. So I joined the Canadian Mounties, you know, the cat-police on horseback. That was great fun. And I had a lovely red uniform and that special Mountie hat they wear, the one with the wide brim. Made me feel really important. I felt like I was making a contribution, catching criminal-cats in the Rockies. But although I was very successful, I only stayed there for a year. It was freezing cold over there. I couldn't wait to get back to somewhere warm. I had a large pot of savings, mostly from snooker prize money, gruff gruff, so I bought a bar in the South of Spain. A lot of hard work that was, and no money to be made."

"Where was that?" asked Stanley.

"In Fingerilla, not far from Catbella. Anyway I'd been there about six months, gruff gruff, when a cat walked into the bar and introduced himself to me. He said that he'd heard of my exploits with the Canadian Mounties, and asked me if I would be interested in working for Customs and Excise as a drug sniffer." Steve was wagging his tail ten to the dozen, but still up and down, not from side to side.

"I thought it would be an interesting challenge," Steve continued, "so I sold up the bar and came back to England. They employed me at the docks in Dover, gruff gruff. Although I say it myself, I was the most successful sniffer dog Customs had ever employed. I was responsible for cracking that big Columbian smuggling ring last year. The drugs had a street value of ten million cat-euros, gruff gruff. Sorry, Christine, I need to go to the toilet before we go out." Steve turned back to the house and went indoors.

"Where on earth did you get that dog, Christine?" asked Stanley, a look of amazement on his face.

"From the RNIBC, the Royal National Institute of Blind Cats. They're a wonderful charity. But I'm thinking of sending him back."

"Why?" said Stanley in a shocked voice. "I've never come across such a fantastic dog. Not many dogs speak cat-lingo for a start. It's just amazing that he's achieved so much in his life. He's a really special dog. Why would you want to get rid of him?"

"He's such an awful liar, Stanley .... gruff gruff!"

The Same Day

Having left Colourful Christine and her "colourful" Guide Dog, Stanley walked briskly down to the harbour, and along the seafront promenade to the Sea View Cafe. Although it wasn't snowing, there was a lot of snow still lying, making the ground underpaw treacherously slippy. He climbed the stone steps to the first floor level, where the cafe jutted out over the road. He nodded a good morning greeting to Wanda, who was on waitress duty as usual.

He chose one of the window tables and ordered the Sea View Special Breakfast and a pot of tea. He had picked up a copy of the Cat-Haven Chronicle at his local newsagents. He laid it flat on the table and read the front page ....

THE CAT-HAVEN CHRONICLE

Published by Sky-Cat Enterprises
Wednesday 14th December
1 Cat-Euro

SHAME OF WEALTHY POLITICIAN-CAT

While the whole of Cat-Haven-on-Sea is mourning the untimely death of Bosun Brian, the former Harbour Master-cat of Brixcat Harbour, a curtain of shame has descended on our town. Sir Lancelot Smiles-a-Lot, 47, your town's elected representative in the Cat House of Commons at Catminster, marched unannounced into this newspaper's offices yesterday. This pompous, puffed up parrot of a cat showed his true colours and his total disregard for the cat-public, which he pretends to serve. Quite disgracefully he tried to influence this newspaper's editorial policy. And not in the interests of the cat-public, but in his own shameless self interest. His attempt to bribe this newspaper into giving prominence to a piffling robbery on his swanky, overpriced boat, currently moored in Brixcat Harbour, was disgusting. His pathetic opinion that the minor inconvenience on board his boat was more important than the sad death of one of our respected citizen-cats left us speechless. But not for long!

Let us put the record straight Sir Lancelot Smiles-a-Lot. **Your minor inconvenience is NOT more important!**

Let us further point out that this newspaper will not take up your squalid request. Or was it a demand?

It is our view that this tedious, tiresome, some would say tainted, toad of a cat, should be kicked out at the next General Cat-Election. This newspaper will actively campaign against him.

It is our fervent hope, that when he reads this article, Sir Lancelot Smiles-a-Lot **will not be smiling!**

But Stanley smiled when he had finished reading the article, and said to himself, "That'll take the wind out of his sails!"

At that moment Wanda came towards his table and placed a huge plate of food in front of him – two free range fried eggs, two pork sausages, two rashers of crispy back bacon, mushrooms, tomatoes, Heinz-Catz baked beans and fried bread.

"That is sooooo cool!" exclaimed Stanley. "That's what I call a breakfast."

Wanda smiled happily. "I'll just go and get your toast and a pot of tea," she said.

The Same Day –
Crime Room Meeting

Just over an hour later Stanley was seated at his desk in the Cat-Haven Cat-Police station.

Derek came in and sat down on one of the visitor chairs. "Did you see this morning's Cat-Haven Chronicle, Stan?"

"Yes I did, Chief. That'll give him something to think about!"

"It certainly will, and it serves him right" said Derek. He was as pleased as a cat sitting at a table with an extra large bowl of cream in front of him! He looked at his mickey-mouse watch. He'd forgotten that it didn't work. As usual it said ten to two. "Is it nearly time for the ten o'clock meeting, Stan?"

"It is, Chief. Let's go."

"But I've only just sat down, Stan. I need a rest."

Stanley shook his head from side to side. "So .... why was it you came into my office, Chief?"

"To go to the meeting in the Crime Room of course." Suddenly Derek realised what Stanley was getting at, and he grinned foolishly. "OK, Stan. You win!"

In the Crime Room, Jack was standing on top of his desk, with a cluster of cats surrounding him. They were all smiling, and looking happy.

"Ok," said Jack, "I've got a question for you, Cyn."

Cynthia sat forward eagerly. "What's the question, Jack?"

"Will you remember me tomorrow, Cyn?"

"Of course I will, Jack."

"And will you remember me in a week?"

Cynthia frowned. "Yes, Jack."

"All right, but will you remember me in a year?"

"I don't understand this, Jack. You know I'll remember you in a year."

"Knock, knock," said Jack suddenly.

Cynthia looked puzzled. "Who's there?" she said.

"Have you forgotten me already, Cyn? I thought you said you'd remember me. Ha! Ha! Ha!"

Cynthia looked blank for a moment. While all the other cats in the Crime Room laughed. And then the cat-euro dropped. "Oh, I get it. Ha, Ha! I fell into that one Jack!"

"You are stupid, Cynthia," said Stephen cruelly, without even looking up from his book, *The Squirrel's Role in Modern Society.*

"Here's one for you, Stephen," said Jack quickly. "What word do *you* always spell incorrectly?

This time Stephen looked up, and gave Jack a look full of disdain. "My spelling is perfect," he said. "I don't spell *any* word incorrectly."

"Yes you do," said Jack triumphantly. "It's 'incorrectly'! Ha" Ha! Ha!"

There was plenty of laughter. Marmaduke jumped up and punched the air. "Good one, Jackster."

Jack grinned broadly. "Since you weren't clever enough to see that one coming, Stephen, and you pretend you know loads of stuff about squirrels, can you answer this one. What's the difference between a squirrel and a chocolate pudding?"

"I don't know and I don't care," said Stephen returning to his book.

"Tammy," said Jack, "next time we've got a chocolate pudding for dessert, can you ask Greta to put a squirrel on Stephen's plate instead, 'cos he won't know the difference! Ha! Ha! Ha!"

There was uproar in the Crime Room. Everyone enjoyed laughing at Stephen.

Before the laughter had died down, the door to the Crime Room opened to reveal Derek and Stanley in the doorway. They realised that Jack had been telling jokes as usual, but at least, thought Stanley, all his cats were in a good mood. Stanley came into the room first, with Derek a few paces behind him.

Derek forgot to close the door. This was a terrible mistake!

Moments later two little kittens raced into the room. Snugsy and Bugsy were out to have some fun! Greta's kitten-sitter had cried off this morning at the last minute. Apparently she had slipped on a banana skin and fallen down the stairs. She had twisted an ankle, and was in a lot of pain, even though she'd taken a couple of Ibucatfen tablets. At what was virtually no notice at all Greta had been unable to find a replacement. This meant that she had no choice but to bring her kitten twins, Snugsy and Bugsy, into the office with her. Once when they were terribly young, and still wearing nappies, they had both had a rather smelly accident. At exactly the same time – being as they were twins!

The kittens raced round the room a few times before stopping in front of Jack's desk. Snugsy leaned towards Bugsy and whispered in his ear. They both grinned, then high fived each other, their faces betraying their mischievous intentions! They raced over to Derek and with perfect timing, they jumped together and clung on to his trousers, just above the knee. Snugsy on the right trouser leg, Bugsy on the left. Their razor sharp claws penetrated the fabric and broke the skin on Derek's legs. He miaowed in pain and tried desperately to throw them off. But they clung on as if their lives depended on it. The cats of the Cat-Haven Cat-Police howled with laughter as Derek struggled in vain to release himself from Snugsy and Bugsy.

"Ok ...... now!" shouted Bugsy. Both kittens let go at the same instant, their claws puncturing and scraping Derek's legs on the way down. Derek yelped in pain once more, and bent down to give his legs a rub.

"And ...... again!" This time it was Snugsy who shouted. They both launched themselves into the air, and landed on Derek's shoulders. Bugsy on the left, Snugsy on the right. Their claws were out, and they clung on to Derek's fleece. Cheers broke out in the Crime Room. Even Stanley couldn't help himself, and he laughed out loud.

Derek was purple in the face by now and flailed his paws, trying to dislodge the kittens. But with no success.

"Oh no!" came a shout from the doorway. It was Greta. She had been busy in her office on the ground floor, typing up correspondence on her computer, when she heard the cheering from upstairs in the Crime Room. With a feeling of utter horror, she saw that her kittens were not tucked up fast asleep in their comfy bed next to Greta's desk. She just knew that the rumpus from upstairs was down to Snugsy and Bugsy!

"Snugsy! Bugsy!" she cried. "Get off Chief Inspector Dimwit. Right now!"

Snugsy looked at Bugsy, and Bugsy looked at Snugsy. They both nodded their heads. At the same moment both kittens sank their teeth into Derek's ear lobes, and bit down hard. Derek screamed in pain. Marmaduke waggled his ears in sympathy. As the kittens let go they drew blood from Derek's ears, and their claws ripped a huge hole on either side of Derek's fleece. And to make matters worse, his blood dripped onto his fleece, which by now was almost ruined!

Snugsy and Bugsy walked casually over to their mother and stood in front of her, their faces a picture of innocence. There was more applause from the assembled cats, as Derek looked on, trying to slow down the flow of blood from his ears. His final humiliation was when Snugsy and Bugsy turned round to face their audience, and with perfectly straight faces, bowed almost in half. Thunderous applause broke out, and Derek wanted the ground to open and swallow him up!

The Same Day – Crime Room Meeting

"**O**k, cats," said Stanley taking up a position by the Incident Board.

Jack dug Marmaduke in the ribs. "Oh, oh. I feel a poem coming on!"

Stanley looked round the room until he had the attention of all his cats. And then he began ....

"It's fun to watch the kittens play.
It's good to smile and laugh and clap.
But do not to fall into the trap
And think it's all we do each day.
For it will cause us all some grief
If we do not find the Harbour thief!"

There was plenty of laughter, and a sprinkling of applause.

"It's time to update ourselves on where we are in

the case," continued Stanley. "Let's hear from Pamela and Katie on their visit to Brixcat Harbour."

Pamela and Katie looked at each other for a moment or two, and then Katie stepped forward, opening her notebook. "Well," she started. "First of all we went to see Eberneezer the Sneezer."

"Did he sneeze all over you, Sis?" interrupted Jack. Stanley gave Jack a severe look, and shook his head. Jack was not in the least put off, and he gave Katie a huge wink, turning his head so that Stanley couldn't see. Or that was what he thought. Stanley did see the wink, and the slight smile that played on Katie's lips. He couldn't help but smile inwardly, but his face betrayed no such emotion.

Katie ignored Jack's comment and carried on with her report. "He told us that he *didn't say* that he thought Bert had killed Bosun Brian. What he *did say*, was that he *wouldn't be surprised* if he had done it. He said that Bert was very bitter that Brian had got the top job. It seems that at the time the previous Harbour Master-cat retired, Bert was already the Assistant Harbour Master-cat, and thought that he should have got the top job automatically."

"Gives him a massive motive for getting rid of Bosun Brian, if you ask me," said Derek.

Marmaduke nudged Jack in the ribs. "I didn't hear anyone ask him, Jack, did you?" Jack grinned. Fortunately for Marmaduke, Derek didn't hear him.

Stanley noticed that Derek's interruption had

confused Katie, and she didn't know whether or not to continue. She was on the point of sitting down when Stanley intervened. "Go on, Katie," he said.

"He also claimed that Bert was responsible for spreading rumours that Brian had bribed the Mayor, and that was why he had got the job."

"That's outrageous!" spluttered Derek. The Mayor's my c-c-c-c-cousin. There's no way he would take a b-b-b-b-bribe. It's outrageous! That Bert's obviously a liar as well as a thief and a m-m-m-m-m-murderer!" Derek had gone purple in the face, and in an attempt to calm down he started to lick his fur furiously.

Stanley raised his eyebrows and winked at Katie, encouraging her to continue.

"There is one other significant thing," she said. "Bert told Eberneezer that he and Brian had had a huge bust up which led to punches being thrown. Or at least, Brian punched Bert who ended up with a massive black eye. Eberneezer thinks that this happened the day before the murder. Bert wouldn't tell Eberneezer what they had argued about, but he did say that he told Brian that if he ever said it to him again, he would kill him." Katie glanced at Pamela. "I think that's all, isn't it Pam?" Pamela nodded. "I'll let Pam take over," continued Katie, "and tell you what we found on the yacht." She sat down.

"Thank you, Katie," said Stanley. "That was a concise, clear report. Well done!"

Pamela stood up, swishing her tail. "The first thing to report is that we established that Katie was right about the boathook. It *does* come from the Flower of Catminster. There were several boathooks on the yacht with the same numbering system. We found two of them, more or less straightaway. One had **FCBH04** on it, and the other one had **FCBH07**."

"Excellent," said Stanley.

"There was no sign of an anchor anywhere on the boat. However, there was a length of chain, about a metre long, with nothing on the end of it. We both thought that it was where an anchor might have been."

"It does suggest the possibility that both the boathook and the anchor were taken from Sir Lancelot's yacht," said Stanley.

"We searched the yacht thoroughly," continued Pamela, "but there was nothing obvious that Jack and Marmy might have missed. Curiously, when we were in the master bedroom we found a scrap of paper that was probably lying under a newspaper. Our guess was that perhaps it was inside the newspaper, and that's why the forensic cats didn't find it." Pamela produced the scrap of paper and passed it to Stanley. "What could it be, I wonder," said Stanley, and passed it to Derek, who looked at it blankly.

2365

NITION

ifles.

llets.

ite.

"There was one thing that did surprise us. When we showed Ship-Shape Shane the photograph of the boathook, he claimed that he had never seen one like it. In view of the fact that he's responsible for the boat when it's in the harbour, it's obvious he must have been on it a number of times. That being the case, wouldn't he have seen those boathooks?" Pamela left the question hanging in the air.

"And a very interesting question too," said Stanley thoughtfully. "And if he's lying ..... why?

The Same Day –
Crime Room Meeting

"Let's hear from Jack and Marmy next," said Stanley.

Marmaduke was busy eating a piece of toast and marmalade, and with his mouth full, he waved his paw at Jack in a "you do it, Jack" gesture.

Jack grinned. "Since Marmy's a bit busy at the moment ..... let me bring you all up to date. We can tell you that the key that was found on the boat *does fit* the front door of the Splash Splosh offices. I'll leave the Sarge to tell you where we go from here. As far as Mackerel Mike is concerned we can reveal that he flew to Tenerife the day after the murder. He went for one week on an 18-30 Cat-Club holiday to Playa de Las Americas. According to the travel agent he booked the holiday at the last minute. Later in the afternoon of the day of the murder. That alone seems a bit suspicious to me. He's due to fly back on EasyCat airlines arriving at Catwick airport late tomorrow evening. We got the information from the Thomas-Cat Travel shop in the centre of town. Do you want us to pick him up when he gets back, Sarge?"

"The Chief and I will think about that, Jack," said Stanley, careful to make sure that the younger cadet-cats appreciated Derek's role in the cat-police force. Although Stanley made most of the decisions, he was always careful not to make it obvious. "I think Tammy has a couple of things to tell us." Stanley smiled encouragingly at Tammy.

"Yes Sarge," Tammy began confidently. "We've had an answer back from Vodacat on Bosun Brian's mobile phone calls, and we can now definitely confirm that the original phone call to the cat-police station was made from Bosun Brian's mobile. It doesn't guarantee that he was the one who made the call, but it seems likely."

Just at that moment Vacant Vincent suddenly shot to his feet and let out a frantic miaow. "Sarge, Sarge," he cried, "I need to go for a poo! It's urgent!" Without waiting for a reply Vincent hitched up his trousers and literally ran to the door. Just before he got there, Apple Pie Annie came strolling in, clutching a blue folder. Vincent clattered into her, knocking her sideways and sending her folder flying. Vincent was normally a very polite cat, but in his state of extreme need he didn't even think of apologizing to Annie. He just raced off in the direction of the toilets.

"Wow!" exclaimed Annie, down on all paws

picking up the contents of her folder that had spilt out onto the floor. "Vinnie was in a hurry. Guess I don't need to ask why!"

Several cats laughed and Annie smiled as she put the last pieces of paper into her folder. "I've got something interesting for you, Stan," she said.

"News on the pawprints?" queried Stanley.

"Sure." Annie pulled out two pieces of paper from her folder. "As you know, there were loads of pawprints all over the yacht. We've eliminated most of them as belonging to Sir Lancelot, as you'd expect. There are six different prints that we can't identify. They're not in the pawprint database, so we're really at square one there."

Derek groaned and Stanley clucked his tongue in disappointment.

"It's not all doom and gloom, guys," said Annie. "I managed to get one good print on the painting which hung over the safe in Sir Lancelot's bedroom. It's a definite match with the pawprint that was on the boathook. It doesn't necessarily prove anything but at least it suggests the strong possibility that the robbery on the yacht, and the murder, were committed by the same cat. Sorry it's not better news."

"Well at least it's better than a slap in the eye with a wet fish! Do you have anything else on the prints, Annie?"

"Well, I don't really like to guess, and I can't give this as a guarantee, but I would say that they probably belong to one of three breeds. It could be a Norwegian Forest Cat, or a Maine Coon, or a Siberian Forest Cat. If we had the machine they've got over in California, I'd be able to be precise, but your equipment here isn't as up to date as ours in the USA. I also examined the painting very carefully, and there was a small hair attached to one corner. I managed to extract a DNA sample from it."

"That is sooooo cool!" beamed Stanley.

Annie grinned. "I thought you'd like that, Stan."

"There's a new piece of evidence, Annie," said Stanley. "We found it in the master bedroom on Sir Lancelot's yacht." He passed the scrap of paper with the number **2365** on it to Annie, who grasped it in her paw. "I'll run some tests on it, Stan. See if anything turns up."

Stanley turned back to face his cats. "Ok, let's see where all that leaves us. Bert is a black Norwegian Forest cat, and we know that he had a motive for killing Brian."

"Of course he does, Stan. I've said it all along – he's obviously guilty. We have to bring him in here to be interviewed. Take his pawprint and get a DNA sample from him. I know it's him."

"I agree about the pawprint and DNA sample, Chief, but I think we'll surprise him and pay him a visit tomorrow morning. The one I think we should bring in is Willy Splish. Before we do that I'd like to get a search warrant to see what we can turn up in his premises. I still think he's a possible for the robbery. Do we know what breed he is?"

"I think he's a Maine Coon," said Jack, looking at Marmaduke for confirmation.

"I agree," said Marmaduke.

"Well, that puts him in the frame, doesn't it? I was also going to bring in Precious Gemma, because she certainly has a motive. All that insurance money. She was pretty cold about Brian's death too. However, since she's a Turkish Angora, perhaps we'll keep her on ice for the moment."

"She could have paid another cat to do it," said Marmaduke.

There was silence for a few moments while everyone thought about what Marmaduke had said.

Katie broke the silence. "What about Shane?" she said. "He's a Norwegian Forest Cat, and I certainly don't trust him."

"I agree with Katie," said Pamela. "I thought he was decidedly tricksy."

"Mmm," murmured Stanley. "We haven't come up with a motive though, have we?"

"Don't forget Mackerel Mike, Sarge. His disappearing to Tenerife like he did was pretty convenient, wasn't it. And the fact that he booked it in such a hurry makes me think he wanted to escape from the situation. And don't forget, didn't he turn up at the scene, like he'd come from the wrong direction or something? He *must* be a possible."

"True! I think we need to find out what breed he is."

The Next Day –
Thursday 15ᵗʰ December

When Stanley and Derek arrived at Brixcat Harbour they were greeted by Nosey Nathan, whose nose looked even bigger than it had done previously.

"Tell Bouncing Bert that we're here," said Derek rudely. "He's expecting us."

Nosey Nathan went back inside his booth, picked up the telephone and spoke into it rapidly. As he came out of the booth he tripped over the telephone flex, and fell head first onto his nose.

"Not exactly a surprise," said Derek to Stanley. "That cat's nose seems to be drawn like a magnet to every hard surface around. I've never known such a clumsy cat!"

Nathan picked himself up and gingerly felt his nose with one of his paws. "He said to go up to his office. I think you know where it is."

* * * *

"Presumably you're the top cat now?" said Derek as soon as they had all sat down in Bert's new office, the office of the Harbour Master-cat of Brixcat Harbour.

"Temporarily," replied Bert. "As the Assistant Harbour Master-cat I have taken on that responsibility until a new top cat is appointed."

"Presumably you're hoping to get the job, Bert," said Stanley.

"Of course I am. I'm the obvious choice."

"We've heard," continued Stanley, "that you thought that you were the obvious choice when Bosun Brian got the job."

"I was. And I should have got the job. After all I was second in command then, just like now."

Derek took up the questioning. "We also heard that you spread sneaky rumours that Bosun Brian bribed the Mayor in order to get the job. What do you say to that?"

"It's not true."

"That's not what we heard."

"Let's turn to something else," said Stanley. "We also heard that you had a huge fight with Bosun Brian a few days before his murder."

"You can't say that isn't true," added Derek. "We know you had a black eye!"

"Yes we did have a fight," replied Bert simply.

"What about?" asked Stanley.

"It was a private matter."

"Nothing is private where a murder has been committed," said Derek. "Why did you fight?"

Bert hesitated, trying to decide whether or not to tell the truth. Eventually he spoke. "He accused me of stealing the petty cash."

"So you *are* a thief," said Derek dramatically. "And did you also rob Sir Lancelot's safe?"

"I'm not a thief. I didn't steal the petty cash, and I didn't rob Sir Lancelot's safe."

"Why do you think Bosun Brian accused you of stealing the petty cash?" asked Stanley. "It seems rather odd for work colleagues. Did you have a bad working relationship with Bosun Brian?"

"We put up with one another. We certainly weren't friends."

"But why did he accuse you of stealing the petty cash?" insisted Derek.

"Well, my son is at Catbridge University, and he got into debt. Spent too much on his credit cards. I had to find a lot of money to pay off his debts. Brian knew this. Foolishly I'd mentioned it to him. I guess he thought I needed money. I was very angry about being accused of such a thing."

"Didn't you threaten to kill him because of it?" said Stanley.

Bert was flustered. "I can't remember," he said.

"According to Mackerel Mike," said Derek, "when he asked you about the fight you'd had with Brian, you told him that if Brian ever did it again you would kill him."

"I suppose I might have said something like that. But it was just talk. You've got to believe me. I would never kill another cat."

"I bet you've killed a few birds in your time, though," said Derek, a grin all over his face.

"Well, that's different. All cats kill birds. Apart from football it's our main sport. You know that. *You* kill birds. Every cat does. You can't beat toying with a bird before you kill it. It's sport!"

"Is there anything you'd like to tell us before we go? Anything that might help our investigations?" asked Stanley.

"I can't think of anything," said Bert, at last feeling relieved that the grilling he'd been getting was about to be over.

"Ok," said Stanley, getting to his feet. "We'd like you to come down to the cat-police station in Cat-Haven so that we can take your pawprints. We'd also like a DNA sample. Any time in the next twenty four hours will do."

Bert visibly blanched, his black face turning pale. "Why is that necessary? And anyway don't you have to have some sort of warrant or something?"

"The reason why," said Derek pompously, "is none of your business. It's cat-police business. And no we don't need a warrant. We're asking you nicely to come down to the station at your own convenience, provided it's in the next twenty four hours.

If you prefer we can arrest you and drag you out of here in pawcuffs right this minute!"

"That won't be necessary," said Bert, an apology in the tone of his voice. "I'll do it tomorrow morning. I've got a busy afternoon and evening today."

"Not much doubt about it, Stan," said Derek as soon as they were outside the Harbour Master-cat's office. "Bouncing Bert is guilty of both crimes. It's obvious. He stole the money and the stuff from Sir Lancelot's boat. Brian probably saw him, or suspected he'd done it. Remember he telephoned the copshop to tell us he knew who had committed the robbery. Maybe Bert overheard the call, and then he killed him. As he admitted himself, they didn't get on. I've got a nose for these things!"

"You could be right, Chief. Let's see if his pawprint and DNA tell us anything."

The Same Day

S tanley and Derek walked back down the flight of stone steps. As they passed the security booth they saw that Nosey Nathan was on the phone. He was clearly having an animated conversation with another cat. He was gesticulating wildly, his paws whirling around his head as if he was some sort of demented windmill.

"It would be fun if he caught his nose with one of his paws," grinned Derek, "and punched himself in the face!"

They passed the booth and walked along the street leading to the far side of the harbour, the wonderful smell of the sea delighting their senses. Stanley took a deep breath, drinking in the aromas, as they passed the kiosks selling all sorts of fish and shellfish. Walking towards them was a female cat who smiled at Stanley, clearly amazed at his bright outfit on a cold winter's day. The trousers he was wearing were a sunshine yellow, with a sprinkling of red spots. If anything his waistcoat was even brighter, a crisscross pattern of blue and green triangles with orange lapels. And a vivid purple bow tie, with a small red and yellow rosette on both sides, perfectly finished off his outfit.

Shortly they came to the bright blue door of the Brixcat Yacht Club. It was shut. Derek hammered on the door with his paw. There was no answer.

Stanley looked through the huge glass window into the office. There was no cat anywhere to be seen. He checked his watch. They were ten minutes early for their appointment with Ship-Shape Shane. "Obviously he's not here yet," he mumbled, more to himself than to Derek. "I suppose we'll have to wait."

For the next twenty minutes Derek and Stanley strolled up and down the harbour, spending a few minutes admiring the Golden Hindcat, the replica of Sir Francis Drakecat's famous ship.

"Let's check with Nathan, Chief," said Stanley eventually. "See if he can shed any light on the missing Commodore-cat."

Back at the security booth all was quiet. Too quiet in fact. Nosey Nathan was nowhere to be seen. "Where on earth is that cat!" said Derek angrily. "He's supposed to be providing the security for the administrative part of the harbour."

"Not very good," said Stanley.

"You could say it's a catastrophe!" grinned Derek.

At that moment Nathan appeared at the top of the stone staircase. He looked surprised to see the two cat-police standing impatiently by the side of his booth. As he came down the stairs and walked over to the security booth, they could see that blood was dripping from his nose, and he was carrying a bloodied tissue in his paw. "I had to go to the toilet," he said by way of explanation. "It was an emergency. I couldn't wait. I didn't want to pee my pants."

"Don't tell me," said Derek, "you caught your nose in the zip of your trousers!"

"I tripped and scraped my nose on the fire extinguisher in the corridor outside the toilet," replied Nathan sharply, dabbing his nose with the tissue.

Stanley had difficulty keeping a straight face. "We have, or should I say had," he said, "an appointment with Ship-Shape Shane ten, fifteen minutes ago in the Yacht Club office. Do you know where he is?"

Nathan pushed past Derek to get to his booth, almost knocking him down. "You should have asked me before you wandered over there," he said smugly. "I could have told you that he won't be in today."

"But he was expecting us. We made the appointment yesterday. We spoke to him on the phone. It's not good enough. I'm the Chief of the cat-police. I won't be treated like this!"

"Tough!" said Nathan a little too quickly.

Derek glowered at him. "How do you know he won't be in today?"

"He phoned in sick this morning. He's got cat swine flu I expect. He said he was dosing himself up with Ibucatfen tablets."

Pliff!" said Derek in annoyance.

"Did he leave a message for us?" enquired Stanley.

"No."

"Well you tell him," said Derek, "to call the cat-police straightaway. And tell him that Chief Inspector Dimwit takes a dim view of his failure to keep our appointment!" He pulled out one of his business cards. It was really scruffy and scrumpled up. And it was streaked with bits of strawberry jam.

"Is this the only card you've got?" queried Nathan. "This has got jam on it!"

"It's the only one I've got with me, so it'll have to do. Your job is to do as I say, and make sure he rings me when he's back at work. What I had for breakfast is none of your business."

The Same Day

J ack pulled up outside the Cat-Haven County Court. He was driving their brand new van, that had only just been delivered from the manufacturer, Catroën Cars. It was called their Crime-Busting Patrol Vehicle. Prominently displayed was the Cat-Haven Cat-Police slogan, which Jack had made up, *"We catch more than mice!"*

Marmaduke, who was sitting in the passenger seat, unbuckled his seat belt, and got out of the van. He was dressed warmly in a thick coat, was wearing gloves on his paws and on his head the warm Russian fur hat that Vodka Valentina had given him. He saw coming towards him on the pavement a huge cat in a motorised wheelchair, clutching a lead in his paw. A fairly small dog, with only three legs, was running along the pavement on the end of the lead, which was about two metres long. He was parallel with the wheelchair, so that he was able to keep his master in sight. But he appeared to be having trouble keeping up, so fast was the wheelchair travelling. The dog was on the very edge of the pavement by the gutter, and Marmaduke had to stand back and press himself against the side of the van until the dog had passed by. He then strode towards the revolving door, which marked the entrance to the County Court.

Five minutes later Marmaduke returned clutching a piece of paper in his paw. It was a Search Warrant for the office premises of Willy Splish. "Got it," he said as he jumped into the passenger seat.

"Specdoinkel!" exclaimed Jack.

Jack was driving, and on the bench seat behind, sat Studious Stephen and Katie.

"Ok, let's go," said Jack, putting his paw down on the accelerator. "You know something, Sis," he said as they moved away from the kerb, "I think it's time we gave you another name. Let's be honest, Skatie Katie doesn't really suit you anymore, now that you've had to give up ice-skating. You're a police-cat now."

"Maybe," said Katie. "Why, have you got a suggestion, bro?"

"As a matter of fact I have. Me and Marmy have been chatting about it. This was Marmy's idea actually – Kool Kat Katie (all Ks)."

"Good, isn't?" said Marmaduke. "You've got a cool dress sense, and I know that you keep your cool under pressure. You never would have been an ice skating champion if you didn't know how to keep cool."

Jack and Marmaduke couldn't see it, but Katie was blushing furiously. "Thanks for that Marmy. It was very sweet of you. And it's unlike you to be so nice to me, Jack!" she said.

Jack laughed. "I know," he grinned. "Guess I have to look out for my little sister sometimes! So, what do you think?"

Stephen, who was sitting next to Katie in the back seat, looked up from the book he was reading, *Common Diseases in Slugs, Maggots and other Creepy Crawlies,* "If you want my opinion ..."

Jack groaned inwardly, expecting Stephen to say something nasty.

".... I think it suits you."

"So, Katie," said Jack, "what do you think? Can you go with it?"

Katie smiled. "Yes," she said. "I think it's a great idea."

"When we get back to the office, I'll tell everyone else," said Jack. "Can anyone guess whether or not we'll find anything at Willy Splish's place?"

"Difficult to say," said Marmaduke.

"We'll soon find out," said Katie.

Studious Stephen of course said nothing. His nose was firmly planted back in his book.

Jack turned on the car radio.
This is the BBC Cat-News at 11 a.m.
An EasyCat flight from Malaga landed at Catwick

Airport earlier this morning and struck a lorry carrying a full load of bananas, that had strayed onto the runway.

"Oh my gosh!" said Marmaduke as the newsreader-cat paused, and then coughed ....

Er .... I mean the lorry strayed onto the runway, not the bananas.

All four cats in the van laughed. Even Stephen! The newsreader-cat coughed again ....

A catastrophe was avoided when the pilot-cat managed to swerve violently, and avoid a full on collision. The wing of the plane caught the back of the lorry which swung round in a full circle and then turned over. A few of the passenger-cats in the plane were treated for minor cuts and bruises and the pilot-cat was completely unhurt. Unfortunately the lorry driver-cat was squashed under a frightening number of bananas. The rescue crew, which was swiftly on the scene, had great difficulty controlling themselves. The temptation to enjoy a banana sandwich was overwhelming!

Five minutes later, on a cold December morning, Jack turned into Decorators Lane. As they approached Paintbrush House they saw Willy Splish coming out of his office. He locked the door, and was about to climb into his van when he looked up and saw the Cat-Haven Cat-Police signs on the vehicle that was approaching. He hesitated, not sure whether to wait and see what they wanted or whether to ignore them and drive off. Curiosity got the better of him, and he stood at the side of his van. He miaowed and yawned at the same time, a sullen look on his face.

"What do you want, now?" he said aggressively, as the four police cats got out of their van.

"We have a warrant to search your premises," said Marmaduke, slipping the search warrant out of his coat pocket.

"As we told you we would," added Jack.

"It needs four of you, does it? What a waste of public cat-euros!"

"If you're on your way out, all you need to do is to give us access, and you can be on your way," said Jack.

Marmaduke grinned at Willy Splish. "Don't worry," he said, "we'll lock up when we leave."

"If you think I'm going to leave you lot all alone in my premises, you've got another think coming."

"Don't you have a secretary or something?" said Marmaduke.

"She left two weeks ago, and I haven't replaced her yet."

"Can't afford to keep her on?"

"That's none of your business," responded Willy angrily. He turned his back on them and made his way back to the front door of his office. He unlocked the door, and strode into the building. "Do whatever you have to and be quick about it. Some of us have work to do," he said over his shoulder. At the far end of the corridor, he opened the door to the tiny kitchen. He filled the kettle half full from the cold tap over the sink, and plugged it in to the electric socket. As he did so, Marmaduke came into the kitchen behind him. Pointedly Willy Splish took one mug out of the wall cupboard, and put four spoons of sugar and a tea bag into it."

"You've got a sweet tooth!" said Marmaduke with a grin. "Not offering us a cup of tea?"

"I don't run my business to provide cups of tea to the cat-police. Bring your own tea or go without!"

"Oops! Bit bad tempered are we? Got out of the wrong side of the bed, Willy?" With that Marmaduke left Willy Splish to make his mug of tea.

The four cat-police searched the premises thoroughly for the best part of half an hour, and found nothing of any interest. Jack was on the point of deciding to call it a day, when there was a loud shriek from Stephen. He was in what was in effect a stationery and filing room. It was a small walk-in room, with shelves and filing cabinets, and several cupboards. One section of shelving had numerous tins of magnolia emulsion paint, and white gloss. There was also a selection of paintbrushes and rollers, buckets and dustsheets. Stephen had spent ten minutes in the room, opening every door, every cupboard, every filing cabinet drawer, and checking every inch of the open shelving. At the back of one of the filing cabinet drawers he discovered a small white cotton bag with drawstrings done up tightly. He pulled it out of the drawer and loosened the drawstrings. It was the contents of the bag that had caused him to shout out.

Jack, Marmaduke and Katie came running, and found Stephen with a huge grin on his face. "Being thorough pays off," he said smugly. "Look what I've found!" He upended the bag and tipped its contents onto the table on which sat the photocopier and a printer/scanner. A small pile of red rubies spilled out onto the table top.

"Oh my gosh!" exclaimed Marmaduke.

"Specdoinkel!" exclaimed Jack.

"Awesome!" exclaimed Katie.

"If I'm right," said Jack, "amongst the jewels that were stolen from Sir Lancelot's safe there were quite a lot of rubies. How many are there, Stephen?"

"Five," replied Stephen.

"I think we need to have a little chat with Mr Splish, don't you guys?"

They found Willy Splish in his office, working on his computer. Since there were only two other chairs in the room, the four cat-police remained standing. Jack wasted no time, and came straight to the point. "Mr Splish, can you explain what this bag of rubies is doing in a filing cabinet in your back room?" In a dramatic gesture, Jack emptied the bag of rubies onto Willy's desk. They gleamed and glistened in the rays of the bright winter sun that angled into the room through the slats of the vertical blinds at the window.

There was a look of shock on Willy's face, and his mouth was dry. "I've never seen them before," he whispered.

"If you've never seen them before," said Marmaduke, "then what are they doing in your office? Hidden away at the back of a filing cabinet drawer. In the hope that no-one would ever find them. How do you explain that, Willy?"

"I'm not going to answer any of your questions without my solicitor being present," said Willy bluntly.

"In that case," said Jack, "we'll have to take you down to the cat-police station for further questioning."

The Same Day

When Jack and the others reached the cat-police station it was time for lunch. Naturally they were not going to be delayed when food was on the table, and so they put Willy in a cell and left him there.

Up in the Crime room Tammy was pacing up and down in front of the dining table. "Miaow, miaow, miaow! I'm starving!" she said. "When is Greta serving up the lunch? Why do we have to wait so long. It's not fair!"

"Oh, be patient," said Jack. "We had to put Willy Splish in one of the cells before *we* could even come up here for lunch."

"Do you mean you've brought in Willy Splish?" queried Pamela.

"Absolutely," said Marmaduke. "We found five rubies hidden in a filing cabinet."

"Actually, *I* found them," said Stephen proudly.

"Yeah, well, you don't usually do much except read one of your stupid books!"

"They're not stupid books, Marmaduke. You're the one who's stupid. The books I read are too smart for cats like you."

"What's smart about the toilet habits of a squirrel? Who would be interested in reading that?"

"Well," said Vincent hesitantly, "..... I would."

This took the heat out of the situation, and all the cats in the Crime Room, except of course Studious Stephen, laughed and clapped their paws together. Soppy Cynthia also laughed, but only because everyone else was laughing.

"Why is that funny, Jack?" she said in a whisper.

"Well, you know what Vincent's problem is, don't you?"

"Oh yes, of course. Silly me! Ha! Ha! Ha! You are awful, Jack."

The laughter of the other cats in the Crime Room was cut short when the door opened to reveal Greta, who was carrying a humungous bowl full of spaghetti bolognese. And right behind her were Derek and Stanley. A hungrifying smell wafted into the room, and most of the cats rushed to the table. Derek was the most eager, and he nearly knocked over Katie in his haste to get seated. He picked up his knife and fork expectantly. Stephen sat on the floor and lifted up one leg. He then started to lick his own bum.

"That's disgusting," said Pamela. "We're just

about to have lunch, Stephen. You should have washed yourself properly this morning. Didn't you have a shower?"

Stephen ignored Pamela's rebuke and continued licking his bum.

Marmaduke nuzzled the leg of the table a few times before taking a seat at the table. Tammy, meanwhile, who had been miaowing and complaining about how hungry she was, was strutting up and down. She was making no move towards the table.

"I thought you were hungry," shouted Jack from his seat at the table.

"Greta knows I don't like Spaghetti Bolognese," said Tammy.

"I can't just make meals for you, Tammy," replied Greta. "Some cats are always complaining. I'm just not appreciated round here."

"That's not true, Greta," said Stanley. "We all appreciate you and the lovely meals you prepare for us. And thanks for bringing up the wine from our wine cellar. A nice bottle of Beaujolais should be perfect." Stanley uncorked the bottle and poured out several glasses of wine. Every cat from the rank of Cat-Constable upwards was allowed to have a single glass of wine with lunch. Cadet-cats on the other hand, had to have a soft drink, such as a Cat-Cola, a Six Up or of course spring water.

"Well *she* doesn't appreciate me," said Greta pointing her mouth at Tammy. "Whatever I make, it isn't good enough for Miss Hoity Toity Tammy!" With that Greta flounced out of the Crime Room.

Tammy tossed her head in the air and walked slowly over to the table, where the other cats were already tucking in. She pulled back the one chair that was unoccupied and leaned forward, her nose almost touching the spaghetti that Jack had heaped onto her plate. Tammy sniffed the food, wrinkling her nose as if it was a plateful of dog's muck. Jack winked at Marmaduke. Tammy took one final sniff before tossing her head back, and with her nose in the air, walked slowly away.

"That's one cat-euro you owe me, Marmy," said Jack in a quiet voice. "I told you she'd walk away!"

Jack need not have bothered to keep his voice down, for Tammy was paying no attention to any of her cat-colleagues.

"Doesn't even smell good," she said under her breath.

The Same Day

I t was the normal routine in the Cat-Haven Cat-Police station, for most of the cats to go to the rest and play room after lunch. All cats were entitled to have a cat-nap after lunch, or to play computer games, pool or darts, or to read the papers. Whatever they wanted, in fact. For the cat-police of Cat-Haven-on-Sea were well looked after.

Jack racked up the pool balls, ready for a game of pool with Marmaduke. Pamela switched on the Nintendo Wii. She and Katie were going to have a game of Super Mario Power Tennis.

An hour or so later Jack and Marmaduke sat in the Chief's office and reported to Derek and Stanley on their visit to the offices of Willy Splish. Jack had also brought in the file on Sir Lancelot's yacht. He took out the list of items stolen from the dynamited safe. Amongst the items listed was a quantity of twenty five red rubies.

"Seems pretty positive proof to me," said Derek. "We might as well charge him with the robbery, Stan. There can't be any doubt."

"We need to interview him first, Chief, before we make a decision."

"He's asked for his solicitor to be present before he answers any questions, Chief," said Jack.

"That makes him even more guilty, if you ask me," said Derek, sitting back in his chair. "If he's innocent, why does he need a solicitor?"

"Do we know his solicitor, Jack?" asked Stanley.

"Yes, Sarge. It's Dodgy Dave. Charlie just buzzed up to say that he had arrived. He took him to the cell where Willy Splish is. He told Dave that he had ten minutes with his client before we started the formal interview."

Ten minutes later Willy Splish, and his lawyer Dodgy Dave, were shown into the interview room. Dodgy Dave was a Havana Brown breed of cat. He was quite tall with long legs and a long tail. He was a rich shade of dark chocolate brown all over, and was wearing a flashy, bright purple suit, which seemed more suitable for a fairground than a cat-police station!

Derek and Stanley were already seated at the interview table. Derek got up from behind the table and showed Willy and Dave to the two chairs opposite Stanley. Derek himself went to stand behind the suspect and his lawyer. This is how they liked to conduct their interviews, one of them in front of the suspect and the other one behind.

Stanley turned on the tape recorder and put the microphone to his mouth. "This is Detective Sergeant Stanley Smartpants of the Cat-Haven Cat-Police conducting an interview with Mr Willy Splish at 2.40 p.m. on Thursday 15th December. Also present is Detective Chief Inspector Derek Dimwit, and Mr Dodgy Dave, solicitor for Mr Splish." He switched off the tape recorder momentarily, and picked up the telephone on the table and buzzed the secretary's office. "Greta, could you please bring in a cup of tea for me, one for the Chief, and two others with one spoon of sugar. Dodgy Dave looked at Stanley enquiringly.

"A cup of tea for you, Dodgy, and one for your client," said Derek from behind Dave's back. "We don't usually offer tea to suspects. Particularly if we think they're guilty! But since he's one of *your* clients, Dodgy, we thought we'd break our own rules."

Dodgy Dave smiled. He hadn't realised that by giving Willy Splish a cup of tea, they would have Willy's pawprint on the cup.

"Let's move on," said Stanley. He turned on the tape recorder. "For the record, Mr Splish, can you confirm your name and address please."

"My name is Willy Splish, and I live at 76 Wallpaper Crescent."

Derek sniggered. "You don't have a hang up about your address, do you?"

Stanley gave Derek a nasty look. "Can you confirm that you are the owner of the business Splash Splosh Painters and Decorators?"

"Yes," said Willy. "You splash out the cash, we splosh on the paint!"

"We don't need to hear advertising slogans, Mr Splish," said Derek.

"And you operate the business from Decorators Lane. Is that correct?

"Yes."

"The first thing we want to ask you, Mr Splish, is how a key to your office premises was found on Sir Lancelot's yacht?"

"What key?" said Willy.

Stanley opened the desk drawer and pulled out a white envelope. He opened it and took out a silver, Yale type key. "This key," he said.

"How do you know it's a key to my client's premises?" asked Dave.

"Two of our officers have checked it, and it fits Mr Splish's front door."

"If this is true, like," said Dave, "did your officers use it to enter my client's premises, 'innit?"

"We were most careful not to use it to enter Mr Splish's premises, Dave," replied Stanley calmly. "That's why we called on Mr Splish this morning with a search warrant."

"You haven't answered Detective Sergeant Smartpants' question, Mr Splish," said Derek. "What was it doing on Sir Lancelot's yacht?"

Willy Splish turned round to face Derek. After a few moments of thought he said, "well, I must have left it there when I was working on Sir Lancelot's yacht. Perhaps it dropped out of my pocket. Does it really matter?"

Stanley Smartpants smiled. "Mr Splish," he said, "we think it does matter. You see it was found in Sir Lancelot's bedroom." Stanley opened the desk drawer once more. This time he brought out three sheets of paper. "This," he said waving the papers in the air is the typed report of the interview Cat Constables Jumping Jack and Marmalade Marmaduke held with you in your office on Tuesday this week. You told them ...." Stanley found the part of the report he was looking for. ".... yes, you stated that when you were working on Sir Lancelot's yacht you at no time went into the Master Bedroom. Do you stand by that statement?"

Dodgy Dave shot his client a warning look. "You don't 'ave to answer that question at the present time, Willy, 'innit."

"It's all right, Dave. I do stand by it. At no time did I go into Sir Lancelot's bedroom," said Willy confidently.

"So the key to your premises mysteriously *turned up* in Sir Lancelot's bedroom?" said Derek.

"Perhaps some cat put it there deliberately so I would be a suspect."

Derek laughed. "Is that the best you can come up with?"

Dodgy Dave interrupted. "My client 'as told you that 'e did not go into the bedroom, Inspector. So somebody else must of put it there. Ok?"

Stanley decided to change the subject. "Can you explain, Mr Splish, why a packet containing five red rubies ...." Stanley emptied the rubies on to the interview desk.

"Objection!" interrupted Dodgy Dave. "Rubies are always red, 'innit!"

"You're not in court, Dodgy," said Stanley. "We don't do objections in the cat-police interview room. Can your client explain why a packet containing five rubies was found in his office?"

Willy opened his mouth to speak, but Dave put a paw on his arm. "Mr Splish 'as already told you, like, that 'e aint got no idea 'ow them rubies came to be in 'is office. 'E's never seen 'em before."

Derek jumped in. "He's *got to* explain. "It's evidence against him! He's *got to!*"

"Let me put it like this, Inspector ...."

"It's Chief Inspector," said Derek.

Dodgy Dave ignored Derek's interruption. ".... Let me put it like this, Inspector. On Tuesday you told Mr Splish that you was goin' ter search 'is premises, like, 'innit? So if 'e 'ad anyfink to do with them rubies, like, don't you fink 'ed 'ave took 'em away, like, instead of leavin' 'em there for you to find, like? It don't make sense, 'innit?"

Willy joined in. "They must have been 'planted' there by some other cat. Probably by the cat who stole them in the first place."

Stanley looked thoughtful. And Derek did too.

"Have you had a break in at your offices lately, Mr Splish?" asked Stanley.

"No."

"If you haven't had a break in, then how do you think the rubies came to be "planted" in your office?"

Willy Splish looked blank. "Er ... I don't know."

"How many keys do you have to the front door of your office?"

Willy paused to think. "I had new keys cut a few weeks ago. My key had broken in half when I locked the premises one night, and I called in a locksmith-cat. He had to drill out the lock and replace it with a new one. I was working on Sir Lancelot's boat at the time, and the locksmith-cat brought the new keys over to Brixcat, and left them in the Yacht Club. There were six keys."

"Let me 'ave a look at them rubies," said Dodgy Dave suddenly. He picked up one of them, and took a jeweller's magnifying glass out of his waistcoat pocket. He held up the ruby in his paw and examined it for several seconds. He then repeated the exercise

227

with the other four rubies. He sat back in his chair. He had a smug expression on his face.

"Just as I fought," he said. "I've 'ad quite a lot of experience wiv precious stones .... and if you ask me they're fakes. I'll bet me granny's knickers they was planted on Mr Splish by the real thief, 'innit?"

Stanley looked at Derek and raised his eyebrows. "Interview terminated at 3.15 p.m.," he said into the microphone. He turned the tape recorder off. "We'll look into the question of whether the rubies are genuine or fakes, Dodgy. You and your client can go. If we need to speak to him again we'll let you know. Thank you for coming in Mr Splish." Stanley patted Willy Splish on the back of one of his paws.

I still think he's guilty," said Derek to Stanley after Willy Splish and Dodgy Dave had left the cat-police station. "Sir Lancelot's rubies *were* found in his office."

"If they are Sir Lancelot's rubies, Chief. Anyway, Dodgy Dave did make a valid point," said Stanley. "If you remember, Jack asked to search the place during their first visit on Tuesday, and Willy Splish told him he needed a search warrant. If he *had* hidden the rubies in the office he would have got rid of them, surely? He must have known that Jack would come back with a search warrant."

"Maybe not. Maybe he thought he'd get away with it, Stan."

"At least I've got a DNA sample," said Stanley. He held up the hair he had taken from Willy's paw when he was leaving. "I'll get Annie to check it out, as well as the pawprint from the cup of tea. And we'll get Marmaduke to update the Incident Board."

The Next Day –
Friday 16th December

A large, black cat stepped out from the Arrivals Concourse at Catwick Airport into a bright, sunny morning. But it was cold. Very cold. He had just returned to the UK on an EasyCat Airlines early morning flight from Tenerife. The weather there had been pleasantly warm, and the cold of England made him shiver. He had forgotten to take a warm coat with him for his return, and the jacket he was wearing failed to keep out the biting cold. He wheeled his suitcase towards the bus stop for the Long Stay Car Park.

"That must be him, Stan," said Derek. "He's certainly a Maine Coon, isn't he?"

Stanley nodded, and stepped towards the shivering Maine Coon. "Excuse me, sir, but am I right in thinking that you are Mackerel Mike?"

"Who wants to know?" said the cat unpleasantly.

"The Cat-Haven Cat-Police," replied Derek. "We want to have a word with you about the death of Bosun Brian at Brixcat Harbour a week or so ago."

Mackerel Mike looked neither surprised nor as if he was expecting to be questioned in the street. His face was a mask of indifference. He was a big, shaggy cat, a black Mackerel Tabby with a white neck and white paws. "Can't you see, I've just come back from holiday. Your questions will have to wait. Come and see me next Monday at Brixcat Harbour. I'll be back at work then."

"It doesn't work like that, Mike," said Stanley. "We want to interview you now."

"You can go to hell!" Mike spat out the words, a speck of spittle sprinkling Derek's face.

"Just you mind your manners," said Derek, wiping the spittle from his face. "And your language."

Stanley brought out a set of pawcuffs, and quick as a flash, he grabbed Mackerel Mike's paws and twisted them round his back.

"This is totally out of order," complained Mike bitterly.

Stanley snapped shut the pawcuffs, and held Mike by the elbow. "This way, Mike," he said, starting to walk towards their panda car, which was parked on the double yellow line no more than twenty metres away.

"What about my car?" said Mike. "It's in the Long Stay Car Park. I just can't leave it here."

Derek looked puzzled. "What shall we do, Stan?"

Stanley made an instant decision. "We'll go with Mike to the Long Stay and then I'll drive his car. You can follow us back to the station."

Derek looked puzzled. "I hear what you say, Stan, but I don't get it. Why do we want to catch a train?"

"Not a railway station, Chief! Our station. The cat-police station."

Mackerel Mike tossed his head. "What a dumb cat!" he said scornfully.

"We didn't ask your opinion, Mike," said Stanley. He pressed the car key button to unlock the panda's doors. "Just get in the back seat." Stanley put a paw on Mike's head, pushed him down, and thrust him into the car.

Derek took the wheel and drove them round the perimeter road to the Long Stay Car Park. When they came to Area G, Mackerel Mike took his ticket out of his wallet. He had written down the row and number where his car was parked. It was a blue, brand new Ford Mondeo.

"Nice car," said Derek with an envious expression on his plain black and white face. "Mackerel fishing must be a pretty rewarding business to be in. I wish I could afford a car like that."

"Ok, Mike, give me your key, please," said Stanley.

"You're not driving my car," said Mike. "I don't let just any cat drive my car."

"I understand, Mike," replied Stanley, "but I can assure you that I'm a very good driver. I've driven squintillions of miles. It may not be ideal, but you'll just have to accept it. Look at it this way, Mackerel Mike, it's better than a slap in the eye with a wet mackerel!" Stanley beamed and turned towards Derek. "That was quite a good one, Chief, wasn't it?"

"Yes it was, Stan!"

"It's my car," said Mike sourly. "I don't want anyone else to drive it."

"After the way you behaved when we told you we wanted to ask you a few questions," said Derek, "it's obvious we can't trust you to follow us. You'll just have to put up with my Sergeant driving your car."

The Same Day

"Ok Cynthia," said Jack. I've got a puzzle for you. Your average cat can jump about one and a half metres high. Of course I can jump at least two metres as you know. That cupboard in the Chief's office is about two metres and I can jump up on to that. So ..... why can't I jump through a one metre high window?"

"I dunno, Jack," said Cynthia slowly. "You should be able to. Why can't you jump through a one metre high window?"

"'Cos it's closed of course! Ha! Ha! Ha!"

Cynthia laughed noisily.

"Gather round guys," said Jack. "Me and Marmy have been practising a special trick with a banana."

"Ooh, that sounds exciting," gushed Cynthia.

"It's awesome," said Katie. "I've seen them practising it!"

Jack and Marmaduke jumped up onto the conference table. Marmaduke was clutching a banana in his paw. He waved it around dramatically. Jack, being Jack, took a bow. Then he raised a paw in the air, and counted, one, two, three. On the count of three Jack jumped up in the air. A split second after Jack's feet left the table, Marmaduke threw the banana up in the air. Jack of course was already slightly above the banana, since he had jumped up just before Marmaduke threw it up. A second before the banana reached the top of its flight, about two metres above Marmaduke's head, Jack extended the claws of his right paw. Quick as a flash his claws found the banana skin, and he skilfully peeled back a few centimetres of it. Jack had been careful not to knock the banana sideways, so that it fell back towards Marmaduke on the same path.

"Hey!" shouted Marmaduke as he caught the banana perfectly.

"Hey!" shouted Jack as he landed back on the table.

"One, two, three," counted Jack once more. And once more he leaped into the air, closely followed by the banana. And once again, in mid flight, his claws fastened round the edge of the banana skin and peeled back some more of it.

Cheers and shouts of "Come On!" came from the cats around the conference table. They could now see the banana itself!

With one more throw, most of the banana was on show. More cheers and applause.

"Hey!" said Jack once more. "One, two, three." He leaped upwards for the last time. On this occasion he closed his mouth round the banana, and bit off a huge chunk. He was still chewing it as he landed back on the table. Marmaduke, with a dramatic gesture, wolfed down a large piece of the remaining banana. He then extracted what was left of it from its skin. Like a victorious tennis player throwing his sweatband into the crowd on the Centre Court at Wimblecat, Marmaduke threw first the banana, and then the banana skin into the crowd of cats around the table.

Both Jack and Marmaduke took a bow, basking in the applause that followed.

At that very moment Chief Inspector Dimwit came striding into the Crime Room.

"I thought you lot were up to something," he said angrily. "I could hear the noise you're all making from my office on the other side of the corridor. What's going on?"

Jack was the first to speak. "Me and Marmy have got a very special trick with a banana, Chief. Would you like to see it?" There were lots of shouts and clapping of paws.

Cynthia, who was normally very quiet in front of her bosses, was so excited by the events of the morning that she piped up. "Yes, Chief, it's a fantastic trick. You're going to love it!"

Derek's face started to turn a deep shade of purple. "No, I'm not going to love it," he said. "I'm not g-g-g-g-going to see it! You cats should be working at helping to solve the Brixcat Harbour m-m-m-m-mystery, instead of playing games with b-b-b-b-bananas. Sergeant Smartpants and I have just come back from Catwick airport, and we've brought Mackerel Mike into the station to be interviewed. Why c-c-c-c-c-can't you cats do something useful. Now get back to work!"

The Same Day

S tanley turned on the tape machine in the Interview Room of the Cat-Haven Cat-Police Station.

"This is Sergeant Stanley Smartpants of the Cat-Haven Cat-Police at 12.15 p.m. on Friday 16th December, conducting an interview with Mackerel Mike. Also present is Chief Inspector Derek Dimwit."

Mackerel Mike scratched his nose.

"The first question we would like to ask you, Mike, is why you rushed off after you and Freddie had pulled Bosun Brian out of the sea?"

"I had things to do. I'm a fishercat you know. Once I get back to the harbour with my catch, I have to take it to the Fish Market to sell it."

"We understand," said Derek, who as usual was sitting behind Mackerel Mike, "that you didn't go to the Fish Market on that particular morning."

"No, I didn't. So what!"

"What did you do with the fish, Mike?" asked Stanley.

"I didn't go to the market myself. My cousin went for me. He sold my fish."

"Why?" said Derek

Mackerel Mike turned round in his chair to face Derek. "I had things to do. I've already told you that."

"What was so important, Mike?" said Stanley.

"It's not really any of your business."

"Everything's our business," said Derek pompously, "when a murder's been committed."

"Bosun Brian murdered!" exclaimed Mike, a shocked note obvious in his voice. "I thought it was an accident."

"What makes you think that?" said Stanley.

"Bouncing Bert said that he tripped on something."

"And you believed that!" Stanley stared straight at Mike without blinking. "Or was it convenient for you that he thought that. Because you hit Brian over the head with a boathook, and then pushed him into the sea?"

Mackerel Mike laughed. "You can't be serious."

"I wouldn't laugh if I were you," said Derek. "Murder isn't a laughing matter."

"I realise that, of course. But it *is* laughable to suggest that I killed him."

Stanley continued. "According to Fishercat Freddie, you seemed relieved that Bosun Brian was dead."

"Well, he got that wrong."

"Relieved because you weren't sure that the blow on the back of the head had killed him?"

Mackerel Mike sat back in his chair and crossed his legs. He looked comfortable and completely at ease. "I didn't kill him, and I had no reason to kill him. I hardly ever came into contact with him."

"Freddie told us," said Stanley, "that he was surprised that when you turned up on the jetty, you didn't come from where your fishing boat was moored, but from the direction of the offices."

Momentarily Mike froze, and then he shook his head, as if trying to remember. "I don't know if I did. Is that what Freddie said?"

"Yes."

Mike shut his eyes for a moment. "Wait a minute. I remember now. I was back earlier than usual and I went over to the Brixcat Tea Rooms for breakfast."

"Presumably one of the staff there would be able to confirm that?"

Mike hesitated. "Er .... well .... I don't know. I don't go there very often."

Stanley persisted. "Did you see anyone you know who could confirm that you went there?"

"I don't think so." Mike looked uncomfortable, and a few beads of sweat were evident on his forehead.

Derek asked the next question, causing Mike to turn round. "You would have had to walk past the Security Booth to go to the Brixcat tearooms. I guess Nosey Nathan would be able to confirm that?"

Mike now looked decidedly guilty. He said nothing.

"Well?" asked Stanley.

"I don't remember seeing him," said Mike.

"That's convenient," said Derek. "I wonder if he remembers seeing you? We'll just have to ask him, won't we?"

Stanley changed the direction of the questioning. "You didn't tell us what was so important that you got your cousin to go to the Fish Market for you. Why *did* he go?"

"I wanted to go to Thomas-Cat Travel to see if I could book a holiday to go somewhere warm for a week. I was fed up with being out at sea every morning in the freezing cold. What's wrong with that?"

"So soon after one of your cat-colleagues was murdered?"

"Sergeant, he wasn't a cat-colleague. I thought it was an accident. And anyway I had already made the decision to have a holiday. The fact that one was available the next day was just a coincidence."

Stanley picked up the telephone and punched in an internal number. "Annie," he said when the phone was answered, "can you please come to Interview Room One. I want to extract a DNA sample and a pawprint from a cat who is helping us with our enquiries."

"Why do you need a DNA sample from me?" said Mike indignantly.

Derek answered. "It's normal cat-police procedure."

"It's nothing to be concerned about, Mike," said Stanley with a forced smile. "If you are not responsible for the murder you have nothing to fear. In fact it will eliminate you from our enquiries."

There was a light knock on the door, which opened immediately to reveal Apple Pie Annie, wearing a long white coat, and carrying a large black bag.

The Same Day – Crime Room Meeting

I t was three thirty on Friday afternoon, and many of the cats in the Cat-Haven Cat-Police were already thinking of the weekend. Some of them knew they would have to spend the weekend Christmas shopping, buying turkeys and last minute presents. And those who had left it late would be scratching around trying to find a decent Christmas Tree.

"Why have they got to have a meeting this afternoon?" said Tammy in a grumpy voice. "It's not fair!"

"Oh, come on, Tammy," said Jack, all bright eyed and smiling. "We've got to solve the Harbour Mystery case. Marmy's been updating the Incident Board, and the Sarge wants us all to contribute."

A minute later Stanley breezed into the Crime Room, with Derek and Apple Pie Annie following behind him. "Settle down, cats," he said. "The Chief and I want to go through the latest information on the Harbour Mystery case. "Marmaduke, did you manage to bring the Incident Board up to date?"

Marmaduke was eating some toast and marmalade he had just prepared in the kitchen. He was chewing on the last piece, and pointed to his mouth with his paw, indicating that he couldn't speak with his mouth full.

"Come on, Marmaduke," said Derek impatiently. "We haven't got all afternoon."

Marmaduke gulped down the last mouthful. "Sorry, Chief. Yes Sarge, it's fully up to date, including the details from your interview with Mackerel Mike this morning."

Stanley smiled. "Good. Well done. Ok, we'll have a look at it in a minute. First of all let's deal with the latest forensic evidence. Annie, what have you got?"

Apple Pie Annie smiled. "Before I start, Stan," she said, "I must say I just love your outfit, especially those pants!"

Stanley looked pleased. His trousers were mauve in colour with red patterned swirls. His bow tie was the same mauve colour with red curved stripes. As usual he wore a waistcoat. This one was a deep blue with some purple diagonal bands and two red diagonal stripes which were quite broad and matched the red swirls on his trousers. Finally he wore a pair of red and purple ankle socks.

Annie took out her huge blue glasses from her coat pocket, and put them on. She opened her blue folder. "As I've already said we have a pawprint on the boathook that I can now confirm definitely matches the pawprint on the painting that was hanging over the safe in Sir Lancelot's bedroom on the yacht. It still remains my view that the pawprint and the DNA evidence from the painting – remember I extracted a small black hair from the painting, which definitely doesn't come from Sir Lancelot – are from the same cat. And of course, it is still my view that all these bits of forensic evidence come from one of three breeds of cat. A Norwegian Forest, a Maine Coon or a Siberian Forest cat. I have one other bit of significant news."

Stanley, Derek and the other cats sat up expectantly. Something new was about to break.

"The piece of paper with the number **2365** and the word **NITION** on it ...." Annie paused and looked round. She saw that she had the full attention of every cat in the room. Or almost every cat!

"Oh, no," shouted Vincent. "I'm so sorry, Sarge, but I need to go for a poo!"

"Pliff!" said Derek angrily. "For goodness sake, Vincent! Can't you control yourself?"

"It's not my ......" Vincent was already running towards the door. "...fault," he cried, and rushed out of the room.

Jack turned towards Marmaduke and whispered

in his ear. "When you've gotta go .... you've gotta go!"

Marmaduke laughed and Derek gave him a filthy look. Jack got up from his chair and went over to close the Crime Room door, which Vincent had left wide open in his headlong rush to the toilet.

"I seem to have an unfortunate effect on Vincent," smiled Annie. "As I was saying," she continued. "There's a new piece of evidence. There is a clear pawprint on the **2365** piece of paper found in Sir Lancelot's bedroom. And ....." Annie paused once more. ".... it matches the pawprint on the painting!"

"Specdoinkel!" said Jack.

"Oh my gosh!" said Marmaduke.

"Awesome!" said Katie.

"That is sooooo cool!" said Stanley.

"It's urgent that we get the pawprints and DNA from *all* the suspects," said Derek. "What about Bouncing Bert?"

"He came into the station this morning," said Annie. "I have his pawprints and a DNA sample. I should know by Monday whether he's a match. I'm also working on Willy Splish and Mackerel Mike. Hopefully one of the three will match what we have."

"Thanks a lot, Annie," said Stanley.

"You're welcome, Stan. I'll get back to the lab and continue working on the stuff I've got." Annie gathered up her papers and stuffed them back into her blue folder.

* * * *

"Marmaduke, can you add these facts to the Incident Board, please," said Stanley. "Bert and Mike's pawprints and DNA samples, and that the pawprint from the **2365** piece of paper matches those on the boathook and the painting. It's certainly beginning to look, more than ever, like both crimes were committed by the same cat."

"Sure thing, Sarge," replied Marmaduke, getting up from his chair and walking over to the Incident Board. He pulled a pen out of his shirt pocket and wrote on the board for a few minutes. He then stood back so everyone could see the board. "I've put a smiley in front of them, Sarge, so we'll know that they're the latest pieces of information."

All the cats of the Cat-Haven Cat-Police who were in the Crime Room turned their attention to the Incident Board.

CASE: 878/879: The Harbour Mystery

Murder of Bosun Brian, Harbour Master-cat at Brixcat Harbour

Theft from Flower of Catminster Yacht, owned by Sir Lancelot Smiles-a-Lot

SUSPECTS & OTHERS   **Last updated:** 16th December

SUSPECTS - MURDER	BREED	INFO. TO HAND	MOTIVE	DNA	PAWPRINT
Bouncing Bert Assistant Harbour Master-cat	Norwegian Forest Black	Suspected liar: Had fight with Bosun Brian and threatened to kill him. Accused of stealing petty cash – money problems (paying off son's debts)	To Get Top Job As Harbour Master-Cat **Prime Suspect**	☺ Pawprint DNA sample Awaiting analysis	
Mackerel Mike Fishercat	Maine Coon Black	Went to Tenerife for 7 day holiday. Claims to have gone to Brixcat Tearooms for breakfast, but no alibi. Suggested Mike was "relieved" that Brian was dead	No apparent motive	☺ Pawprint DNA Sample Awaiting analysis	
Fishercat Freddie Fishercat	American Black Bombay	Could have paid another cat to murder Brian	No apparent motive		
Precious Gemma Brian's Wife	Turkish Angora White		Life Insurance payout		
Ship-Shape Shane Commodore-cat at Brixcat Yacht Club	Norwegian Forest Black	Has key to Sir Lancelot's yacht. Knew about death very soon after it occurred.	No apparent motive		

SUSPECTS- ROBBERY	BREED	INFO. To HAND	MOTIVE	DNA PAWPRINT
Sir Lancelot Smiles-a-Lot	Burmese Brown	Politician-cat. One of his companies owns Flower of Catminster yacht. Cash and jewels stolen from safe in bedroom of yacht	Large Insurance Policy payable if jewels not found	Pawprint
Willy Splish Painter and Decorator	Maine Coon Black	His decorating business seems to be doing badly. Last tradescat to have access to Sir L's yacht. Key to his office found in sir L's bedroom. 5 rubies found at his office.	? Business doing badly - ? money problems Prime Suspect	Pawprint DNA Sample Awaiting analysis

EVIDENCE - MURDER		INFORMATION TO HAND	COMMENTS
Boathook		Found in sea at Brixcat harbour. DNA evidence of blood and hairs of Bosun Brian. Letters FCBH03 on handle - came from Flower of Catminster yacht Pawprint on handle	The Murder Weapon ☺ Matches pawprint on painting
Anchor		Rusty old anchor was attached to boathook to keep it on the sea bed. Anchor missing on Flower of Catminster boat	Suggests that the killer had knowledge of sea and access to anchor and boathook

Cat-Haven Cat-Police   **INCIDENT BOARD**

CASE: 878/879: The Harbour Mystery

Murder of Bosun Brian, Harbour Master-cat at Brixcat Harbour

Theft from Flower of Catminster Yacht, owned by Sir Lancelot Smiles-a-Lot

SUSPECTS & OTHERS   **Last updated:** 16th December

EVIDENCE - ROBBERY	INFORMATION TO HAND	COMMENTS
Yale Key — silver in colour	Found in Master Bedroom on Sir L's yacht. Key to Willy Splish office.	
Pawprint on painting	Found on painting in Master Bedroom on Sir L's yacht	☺ Matches pawprint on boathook
Hair on painting	Black hair found on painting in Master Bedroom on Sir L's yacht	☺ DNA match with pawprint on boathook
Rubies	5 of the rubies stolen from Sir L's yacht found in Willy Splish office.	? could be fakes
Piece of paper - 2365	Found in Sir L's bedroom. ? Torn from a larger piece of paper? 2365 NITION. ifles. llets. ite.	Pawprint ☺ Analysed – Matches pawprint on painting and boathook

250

The Same Day

"How can we have two Prime Suspects?" said Stephen. "Prime means one. The Prime Suspect is the number one suspect."

"Shut up, Stephen," said Derek angrily. "Don't be such a know-it-all."

"Have we got any news on Ship-Shape Shane?" asked Stanley.

"Not really, Sarge," said Jack. "I checked this morning, and he hasn't been in to work. He didn't ring in according to Bouncing Bert. I also spoke to Nosey Nathan and he hasn't heard anything either. They both think that he must be down with cat swine flu."

"Mmm," mumbled Stanley. "Did you get his address, Jack?"

"Yes, he lives in a small cottage up near Cat-Haven Point."

"Good. I think we'll pay Mr Shane a visit. I'd like you and Marmaduke to go and call on him early on Monday morning and bring him into the station."

"I hear what you say, Stan, but what reason for bringing him into the station are you going to give him?" asked Derek. "I mean we don't have any reason, do we? He hasn't got any motive, for one. It's obvious to me that Bouncing Bert is the murderer *and* the thief. He has a motive for both. We just need the proof from Annie. And if he isn't the thief, then Willy Splish is."

Stanley smiled. "I hear what *you say*, Chief. But until we can be sure about that we have to continue checking every possibility. As you just said, we need forensic evidence from *all* the suspects.

"I meant Bouncing Bert," said Derek irritably. "The Prime Suspect."

"Chief," said Stanley, "it's not true to say that Ship-Shape Shane doesn't have a motive. It would be more correct to say that we don't *know* of any motive."

Pamela caught Stanley's eye. "Excuse me, Sarge," she said, a little hesitantly. "I'm not criticising anyone, but there is something about Shane that isn't on the Incident Board. I just wanted to remind everyone about me and Katie's report on our visit to the Yacht Club, and that Shane lied to us about the boathook. When we showed him the photo of the boathook, he said he'd never seen one like it!"

"Yes, I remember that now," said Stanley. "Lying to the cat-police gives us our reason for bringing him in to be interviewed, Chief."

"I suppose so," said Derek. "All right then. Bring him in." Derek managed to make it sound like it was his idea all along!

"Also ...." Pamela continued, "both me and Katie didn't trust him. He had shifty eyes. He's probably guilty."

"Just because he had shifty eyes, Pamela?" said Marmaduke quickly.

"And he had a beard!" snapped Pamela.

Jack and Marmaduke laughed heartily.

Studious Stephen looked up from the book he was reading, *Chinese Cat Medicine in Western Europe, Volume 2.* "When I was at the Cat-Police Training School, we were taught not to make judgements based on appearances."

"Oh, shut up, Stephen," said Jack, rolling his eyes and winking at the other cats in the room. Several of them started laughing.

"Now listen up cats," said Stanley. "This is what I think ....

> *To solve the crime and find the crook,*
> *At ev'ry detail you must look.*
> *And if a cat has shifty eyes,*
> *It often goes with telling lies!*
> *It's only when you look you find a clue,*
> *And I can tell you Stephen that it's true,*
> *You will not find it in a book!"*

****

253

Stephen blushed, and sweat trickled down his face. Jack and Marmaduke did a high five. And seeing that, so did Pamela and Katie. Every other cat enjoyed Stephen's put down. In truth, Stephen was frequently so cruel to all the other cat-constables and cadet-cats, that he didn't have any friends. And everyone enjoyed it when he was put in his place.

"Let's continue," said Stanley. "We haven't discussed Precious Gemma for a while. The motive is still there of course, the insurance payout on Bosun Brian's death. But if she committed the murder, and as a result has come into a substantial sum of money, then she would not have needed to steal the rubies and cash from Sir Lancelot's yacht. Would she?" Stanley paused and looked round the room. None of his cats had anything to contribute so he carried on.

"As you all know, Chief Inspector Dimwit and I interviewed Mackerel Mike earlier today. He wasn't terribly convincing. He told us that he went to Brixcat Tearooms for breakfast, but he can't prove it. He wasn't able to give us the name of any cat who could confirm it. He also claimed that his cousin took his fish catch to Cat-Haven Fish Market, but we're not convinced that he even has a cousin. So there are still a number of question marks against him."

"It could be him, Stan," interrupted Derek.

"Maybe Chief. We have his pawprint and a DNA sample, so that may well tell us something." Stanley continued with his analysis. "Now we come to Willy Splish. When the Chief and I interviewed him, he couldn't explain how the key to his premises came to be found in Sir Lancelot's bedroom. He also couldn't explain how five rubies were in one of his filing cabinets. His solicitor, Dodgy Dave suggested that the rubies in our possession are fakes. Marmaduke, did you take them down to Diamond Lil at Cat Diamonds "R" Us?

"Yes I did, Sarge. Lil examined them thoroughly. It was quite funny, all the time she was examining them she was singing 'Diamonds are a Cat's Best Friend'! She confirmed that they *are* genuine. I also showed her the photograph of the rubies that Sir Lancelot e-mailed over to us. In her expert opinion the rubies we found in Willy's office *are* the same as the ones in the photograph. To be absolutely certain, however, she would need to compare them with the twenty rubies that are missing."

"Which of course we can't do unless we find them," said Stanley in reply. "In any event Willy Splish is claiming that both the key and the rubies were *planted* on him by some other cat."

"That's nonsense!" interrupted Derek. "Nobody's going to believe that! The more I think about it, the more I think he's the guilty cat. His business is doing badly according to Jack and Marmaduke. That's a perfect motive for stealing stuff from Sir Lancelot's safe."

* * * * *

Katie now raised a paw above her head, and looked enquiringly at Stanley. He nodded. "Chief," she began, "why would he leave only five rubies in that filing cabinet? It doesn't make sense. I mean, why would he split them up?"

"Pliff!" exclaimed Derek. "How do I know? It doesn't matter how many rubies he left there. The important thing is that they *were* there. It's either him or Bouncing Bert, I'm certain of it."

It was Tammy's turn to raise her paw, and look over at Stanley.

"Yes, Tammy, go ahead."

"I looked into Sir Lancelot's finances as you asked me to."

"Yes, I'd forgotten about that," said Stanley.

"Well, I made some discreet enquiries at the Cat House of Commons, and the word is that he's in a bit of trouble financially. It seems he's got a huge amount of cat-euros to pay back for expenses he had wrongly claimed. Several cats told me that he's been trying to borrow money."

"That is *very* interesting," said Stanley. "Thank you, Tammy."

"Well that does give Sir Lancelot a motive for wanting an insurance payout on his stolen rubies, doesn't it?" said Jack.

"To sum up," said Stanley. "We have pawprint

and DNA evidence from Bert, Willy and Mike. And we should know in a couple of days if one of them is a match. It only remains to interview Shane, and obviously get his pawprint and DNA. It's always possible of course, that it's none of them, so we must keep an open mind. One other thing we can do is follow up the **2365** piece of paper. I'd like every cat to think about that, and try and work it out. Something tells me it's a vitally important clue!"

The weekend –
Sunday 18th December

Katie got up late on Sunday morning, and was still wandering around in her dressing gown and slippers at midday. She looked at the large clock on her living room wall and saw that it was ten past twelve. She realised that if she didn't hurry she would be late meeting her brother, Jack. She took a quick shower and had a few mouthfuls of Apricot Wheats.

When Katie arrived, somewhat breathlessly, at the Weatherpaws pub, Cats of the Town, in the centre of Cat-Haven, Jack was already sitting at a table with a pint of extra cold draught Guinness in his paw. Spread out in front of him was his Sunday newspaper, the Purrfect Times. He was reading a report on the football match between the Cat-Haven Gooners and Catchester United. The Gooners had won the match 3-2. Much to the enjoyment of the Gooners' supporters, United's star striker, Wayne Spooney, had missed the simple chance to equalise in the last minute. Wayne always played with a spoon taped to his left boot, so that he could perform his favourite trick of "spooning" the ball over the goalkeeper's head. Unfortunately, before the game, he had used the spoon to eat a bowl of a sort of soup concoction, made up of a mixture of marmite and strawberry yoghurt. And since he was a pampered, spoiled footballer-cat he naturally assumed that some other cat would clean his spoon for him. No cat had! When the crucial chance fell to him in the last minute, instead of a simple tap-in with his right boot, he decided to show off, and tried to "spoon" the ball over the goalkeeper's head. But the ball got stuck to the sticky spoon and the chance was lost.

As soon as Jack saw Katie, he jumped up and went to the bar, where he ordered a Malibu and coke for her.

Since it was Sunday the pub offered a traditional Sunday lunch. Jack had roast beef with catradish sauce, while Katie opted for her absolute favourite, roast lamb and mint sauce. Roast potatoes and vegetables were plentiful. Jack hated sprouts when he was at school, but now that he was grown up he really liked them with a roast dinner. Katie thought that he was overdoing it a bit when he decided to have three Yorkshire puddings, and they both had lashings of gravy. After lunch they went for a walk on Torcat beach. Curiously, although it was cold enough to snow, they saw two kittens without coats, playing with buckets and spades, building sandcastles.

Katie now sat at her dining table, with her copy of the words on the torn piece of paper in front of her, trying to puzzle it out. Since the jagged piece of paper had a straight edge on the right hand side and three of the four words had a full stop after them, surely it meant that all the words they had were the end of a sentence.

2365
NITION
ifles.
llets.
ite.

She had decided some days ago that the number at the top of the piece of paper could well be an invoice number. And this would mean that it came from a business of some sort. But what business? What type of business? The only way to establish the type of business would be to work out what the words actually were.

On Friday afternoon Cynthia had suggested that the word 'ifles' could be *'trifles'*, much to the amusement of Jack and Marmaduke. Jack had said, "do you want ice creams with your trifles, Cyn?" No, *'Trifles'* didn't seem very likely! Last night Katie had been watching a cat-movie on TV with lots of fighting and guns and stuff. Recalling this now she suddenly thought that 'ifles' could in fact be *'rifles'*, Cynthia might not have been so far away from guessing part of the puzzle after all!

With this thought in her mind she got up from the table and went in to the kitchen. She thought a nice cup of tea would help her to concentrate on solving the puzzle. She filled the kettle with water and plugged it in. While she was waiting for the water to boil she paced up and down, stopping now and then to head butt one of the kitchen cupboards. She pictured each of the words. She couldn't figure out what 'ite' could possibly be, or 'llets'. She concentrated on the word *'rifles'*. What else could go with rifles? Guns .... pistols ..... revolvers ..... shotguns .... Of course! 'llets' could be *'bullets'*. Rifles and bullets.

She made her tea in one of her favourite mugs, with just a dash of skimmed milk so it was nice and strong. She took it through to the living room and put it on the dining table. With mounting excitement she went over to the bookcase to look for the Purrple Pages, which advertised businesses. She wasn't sure what category to search under, so she looked first of all in the index. And there it was! Right at the beginning .... **Arms and Ammunition**. That was the first word solved too ..... *'ammunition'*. Now she was getting somewhere!

She sat back down at the table, and shuffled through the Purrple Pages until she came to the Arms and Ammunition section. Amongst the adverts she found this:

CAT-HAVEN ARSENAL

For all your armament needs!

- **Firearms** - revolvers, hand guns of all types, shotguns, rifles.
- **Ammunition** - Shotgun pellets, all types and calibres of bullets.

Large Stocks, Competitive Prices,
Discounts for large quantities

1176 Shore Road, Cat-Haven-on-Sea   Tel. 6742
See also our entry under Explosives

Immediately Katie went to the section headed explosives and found the Cat-Haven Arsenal advert. It also solved the final puzzle – 'ite' was probably *'dynamite'*.

Katie was sure that she had tracked down the source of the scrap of torn paper that she and Pamela had found in Sir Lancelot's cabin on board the Flower of Catminster. Tomorrow she would visit the Cat-Haven Arsenal. With a feeling of great excitement she jumped up onto the sofa, made herself as comfy as possible, and turned on the TV. It was Catsomer Murders. Roll on tomorrow, she thought. I wonder what I'll discover?

The Next Day –
Monday 19ᵗʰ December

Stanley had got in early on Monday morning. He knew it was going to be a big day. He knew that it was going to be the day they cracked the Harbour Mystery case. He was wearing his "case solving trousers". He had ordered them online from British Cat Stores on the day he solved the Mackerel Robberies case. That had been back in July when the weather in Britain had been so hot it could have been the South of Spain. So naturally they were light in weight and summery in style. And although the weather now was decidedly cold and unsuitable for summery clothes, Stanley didn't care. The trousers were a bright white cotton with a sprinkling of blue and green fish, a design that seemed completely appropriate at the time the Mackerel Robberies case was solved. His waistcoat had broad green and blue horizontal stripes and yellow lapels. Curiously there was a yellow question mark on one of the blue stripes, roughly where his heart was. A white bow tie with red spots completed the outfit.

Over the weekend, he had taken home with him the notes from all the interviews they had conducted, including notes of phone calls. Straight after lunch on Friday he had asked Greta to make written copies of the Incident Boards. Of course she had grumbled and grumbled about it, but she had done it. He had spent most of Sunday studying everything.

He had started right back at the beginning with the phone call Cynthia had taken from the Harbour Master-cat about the robbery. Late on Sunday evening he had had a breakthrough. He was now convinced that he knew who had carried out the robbery, and who had murdered Bosun Brian. He was sure that one cat had been responsible for both crimes.

He got up from his desk and wandered into the kitchen. He had decided to make himself a mug of strong coffee. As he was returning to his desk the phone rang. It was Cheerful Charlie.

"Hello, Stan," he said. "I've got Katie on the line for you."

"Thanks, Charlie, put her through."

"Good morning, Sarge" said Katie. "Just to let you know, Pamela and I are following up a lead on the Harbour Mystery case, so we'll be a bit late getting in to the office."

"That's OK," said Stanley. "Do you want to tell me about it?"

"I'd rather wait till we've got something concrete to tell you, Sarge. If that's all right?" she added, a little hesitantly.

"No worries. See you when you get in."

No sooner had Stanley put the phone down, than it rang again.

It was Charlie. "I've got Jack for you now."

"Thanks, Charlie."

"Morning, Sarge. Good to know you're in the office nice and early!" Stanley couldn't see the huge grin on Jack's face when he said this, but he could imagine it. Jack enjoyed being a bit cheeky to Stanley when he got the chance.

Stanley couldn't help a smile crossing his lips. "Where are you?" he asked.

"Me and Marmy are sitting in the Crime-Busting Van, outside the Brixcat Yacht Club. So far Shane hasn't turned up. We went to his apartment first but he wasn't there."

"Makes sense," said Stanley. "Keep me updated. Better to call me on the mobile, Jack."

"Will do, Sarge." With that Jack disconnected the call.

Stanley sat back in his office chair and wondered if they had enough evidence to charge the guilty cat. They still had to prove it of course, and that wouldn't be so easy! He hoped that Annie would soon have all the DNA results, and that they would help. But ideally they needed more than pawprints and DNA evidence. And if the test results didn't back up his conclusions as to the guilty cat? What would happen then? He strongly felt that the two most important pieces of evidence were the office key belonging to Willy Splish, that was found in Sir Lancelot's bedroom on the yacht, and the five rubies that were found in Willy's office. Time would tell.

The Same Day

Literally five minutes after Jack disconnected his call to Stanley, Marmaduke nudged him in the ribs. "Here he comes, Jack," he said.

Jack looked up to see Ship-Shape Shane coming towards them. He was wearing a long, crumpled, grey coat that seemed to have all its buttons missing. At any rate it was flapping in the wind. And on his head was a dirty captain's hat. He was carrying a briefcase that was so full it looked as if it would burst open at any second. He was obviously in a hurry, and didn't even notice the Cat-Haven Cat-Police van.

Quickly Jack sent a text to Stanley. *Shane just arrived* was all it said.

"Let's give him a couple of minutes, Jack," said Marmaduke. "See if he does anything suspicious."

"Good idea," replied Jack. "He looks like a cat with something on his mind."

* * * *

They waited for five minutes before getting out of the van and entering the Yacht Club office.

As they walked in Shane was stuffing things into an open suitcase that was lying on his desk. The moment he saw Jack and Marmaduke he hastily slammed the suitcase shut. "Oh, it's you two again," he said. There was a nervous tremor in his voice and a guilty look on his face.

"Going somewhere, Shane?" said Jack.

"Er .... no," Shane said unconvincingly.

"Actually, yes you are," grinned Marmaduke. "To the cop shop!"

"With us," added Jack.

"Why would I do that?"

"Because Sergeant Smartpants wants to have a word with you," said Marmaduke.

"Well, I don't want to have a word with *him.*"

"But we insist," said Jack.

"And I insist that I'm not going to the cat-police station."

Jack looked at Marmaduke, and Marmaduke looked at Jack. They had no need to speak. Quicker than a flash of lightning, well almost, Marmaduke rushed at Shane, grabbed his paws and twisted them round his back. Quicker than a bolt of thunder, well almost .... *or is thunder quick?* .... well, anyway, Jack knew what he had to do, and he pulled out his pawcuffs and fastened them around Shane's paws.

"This is outrageous," screamed Shane, struggling

against the pawcuffs.

"We asked you nicely, Shane," said Jack, "but you chose to ignore our invitation."

"Didn't sound like an invitation to me," spat out Shane, his cheeks reddening as he still fought the pawcuffs.

"That won't do you any good," said Jack. "Just be a good little cat and come quietly."

Marmaduke opened the suitcase. "Just hold on to him, Jack," he said. "I think we should have a little look in Shane's suitcase. See if we can find anything interesting."

Jack took a firm grip on Shane.

"Oh, my gosh!" said Marmaduke with excitement. "What have we here?" He pulled out a small maroon coloured booklet with fancy gold writing on it. "I do believe this is your passport, Shane." Marmaduke riffled through the pages till he came to the photograph page. "As ugly as ever, Shane. Unmistakeably you though!" He turned towards his companion. "Do you think he's planning a trip abroad, Jack?"

"Are you, Shane? asked Jack.

"None of your business!" Shane replied. "Am I under arrest?"

"I think you can definitely say that, Shane. Come on, Marmy, let's shove him in the back of the van. I'll call the office once we've got him trussed up in the van, and tell them to expect us .... with a prisoner!"

The Same Day

Katie was at the wheel of her own car, with Pamela sitting beside her, as they drove along Shore Road, the coast road from Cat-Haven to Brixcat. The familiar voice of the female cat on Katie's satellite navigation system spoke.

"In two hundred yards turn right."

Katie put her indicator on and moved towards the centre of the road. As soon as there was a break in the traffic she turned right.

The Cat-Nav voice spoke again. *"In one hundred yards you have reached your destination."* And then a few moments later .... *"you have reached your destination."*

"Good," said Pamela as the car came to a halt. They had pulled up directly outside a large, imposing warehouse-type building. In large red, illuminated letters were the words **Cat-Haven Arsenal**.

At the reception desk Katie and Pamela showed their warrant cards and asked to see the boss. Groovy Grace, the receptionist-cat, was listening to music through a set of earphones. She pulled them out of her ears and picked up the telephone. "Hi, Fergie," she said, "there are a couple of cool cat-police officers here. If you can spare the time they'd like to see you." There was a short silence, after which she said, addressing Katie and Pamela "can one of you tell me what it's about?"

"Just tell Fergie, that we need to ask him a few questions," said Pamela forcefully. "It's not a request. We're not asking if he can *spare the time*" she continued, "we insist that he sees us right now. Is that clear enough for you?"

"Oops," said Grace with a grin. She spoke into the phone once more. "It seems that they insist on seeing you now, Fergie. They're not very groovy." She put the phone down. "He'll be out in a minute," she said, and then switched on her ipod. Although she had earphones Katie and Pamela could clearly hear the groovy music Grace was listening to. She turned her attention to the computer screen in front of her, and completely ignored Katie and Pamela.

Two minutes later a well fed grey cat, a Tonkinese, appeared in a doorway. "Follow me," he said. "We can speak in the showroom."

Katie and Pamela followed the Tonkinese along a long, narrow corridor, and eventually into a large room packed with firearms of all kinds. Most of them were displayed behind glass in long wall cabinets.

"I'm Firearms Fergie. I'm the owner of the business.

Please take a seat." He pointed to some chairs which surrounded a large mahogany table. "Could I just see some identification?"

Katie and Pamela put their warrant cards on the table and pushed them towards Fergie, who had also now taken a seat.

"I'm sorry if Grace, that's my receptionist-cat, upset you a bit. We get so many salescats calling on us trying to sell us stuff we don't want. You know how it is, I'm sure. She's just trying to protect me, so I can get on with my work. Anyway, what can I do for you, Officers?"

Katie took the copy of the torn scrap of paper from her pocket and passed it to Fergie. "Do you recognise this, Fergie?" she said passing him the piece of paper.

"It looks like something torn from one of our invoices."

Katie looked at Pamela triumphantly.

Fergie picked up the phone. "Grace," he said, "can you ask Megan to bring me in a copy of invoice number 2365." He put the phone down. "Multiplication Megan is our book-keeper. She does all the accounts and invoicing and stuff. She's very efficient, so I don't think it will take long. Can you tell me what it's about?"

Katie was about to speak, but Pamela raised a paw to let Katie know that she would answer the question. "Sorry, Fergie, we can't say more than it's a case we're working on. But I can tell you that it could be important."

CAT-HAVEN ARSENAL	INVOICE No. 2365
1176 Shore Road	
Cat-Haven-on-Sea	
Tel: 6742	

CAT-HAVEN ARSENAL — ARMS AND AMMUNITION

Firearms — revolvers, hand guns of all types, shotguns, rifles.
Ammunition — all types and calibres of bullets, shotgun pellets.
Explosives — detonators and fuses, TNT, gelignite, dynamite.

Name:	Date:
William Sticker	30th November
37 East Road	
Brixcat	

NO.	DETAILS	Amount Cat-Euros
2	Sticks 657 Low Impact Dynamite @ 265.00 Cat Euros	530.00
1	Length 25 metres Fuse Wire @ 6.50 per metre	162.50
	Paid Cash	
	TOTAL	**692.50**

"Would you like to look at some of our range of firearms while we're waiting for Megan?"

Before either Katie or Pamela could reply there was a light knock on the door, and a beautiful Blue Korat came into the room. She was smiling broadly and waving a sheet of paper. "I think this is what you want, Fergie," she said. She handed him the invoice copy.

Fergie looked at it briefly before placing it face up on the table. "Thanks Megan," he said.

Katie and Pamela studied it at the same time. Katie raised her eyebrows. "This looks interesting," she said to Pamela. And then to Fergie. "Does this mean that the dynamite was supplied on November 30th, in other words three weeks ago?"

"Absolutely," said Fergie.

"Is William Sticker a regular customer, Fergie?" asked Pamela.

"No, that was the first time this cat had ever bought anything from us."

"By the sound of it you remember him?" queried Katie.

"I certainly do," smiled Fergie.

"What can you tell us about him?"

"First of all I don't think his name is William Sticker."

"Why not?" asked Pamela.

"When I asked for his name for the invoice, he hesitated for ages. For too long in fact. He was standing by that window, and staring out of it. *That* window," said Fergie, pointing to the far wall.

He got up from his chair and walked towards the window. "Come and look," he said.

Katie and Pamela both looked out of the window. Directly opposite was an empty shop. There were several notices pasted to the shop window.

```
┌─────────────────────────────────────┐
│                                     │
│     BILL STICKERS                   │
│     will be prosecuted              │
│                                     │
└─────────────────────────────────────┘
```

Pamela looked puzzled.

"Haven't you seen that sort of notice before, Pam?" said Katie.

"No, I haven't."

"What often happens when a shop falls empty is that certain cats put up posters, also known as bills, advertising things like concerts or gigs to be held by the likes of the Red Hot Chilli Cats, Cats Aloud or Cat Sheeran, but without the permission of the owner of the shop. In other words it's free advertising. So what the owners of shops often do is to put up their own notice warning that they will take legal action against any cat who sticks posters, or bills, on their shop windows, like for example, 'Bill stickers will be prosecuted'."

"Right," said Pamela. "So he obviously couldn't think of a name to make up, changed Bill to William, and came up with William Sticker!"

"That's how I figured it too," said Fergie, "but after he'd left of course."

"Can you describe him, Fergie?" asked Katie.

"I can do better than that," grinned Fergie. "He didn't realise it, but I took a photo of him on my phone." He took out his Blackberry. "There you are," he said, and turned the phone round so that both Pamela and Katie could see who it was. They both recognised the cat in the photo straightaway.

"Well, well, well!" said Pamela.

"Very interesting!" said Katie.

The Same Day

Ship-Shape Shane sat at the wooden table in Interview Room One. When he had arrived at the Cat-Haven Cat-Police Station Stanley had instructed Charlie to read him his rights. He had not asked for a solicitor. Annie had taken a pawprint and a DNA sample by putting a cotton swab in his mouth.

Stanley decided to soften him up a bit by making him wait on his own for a full hour. During that time he and Derek planned their interview strategy. At last they entered the room. Stanley sat at the table, facing Shane. Derek sat on a chair behind Shane. Stanley turned on the tape recorder.

"This is Detective Sergeant Stanley Smartpants of Cat-Haven Cat-Police conducting an interview with Ship-Shape Shane on Monday 19th December at 11.17 a.m. Also present is Detective Chief Inspector Derek Dimwit."

Stanley opened the questioning. "Shane, did you break into Sir Lancelot's safe on board his yacht?"

"No, I did not."

"We think you did," said Derek from behind Shane's back.

"No, I didn't," said Shane without turning round.

Derek raised his voice slightly. "Look at me when I'm speaking to you, Shane. We think you did."

This time Shane did turn round. "Do you have any proof?" he asked.

"We're asking the questions, Shane," said Stanley. "I had a telephone call from Sir Lancelot a few days ago, during which he accused you of cheating him. His book-keeper-cat had just informed him that you had invoiced Sir Lancelot twice for the same work on several occasions over the last six months."

"That's rubbish," said Shane crossing his legs, trying to make himself comfortable. "Sir Lancelot has never mentioned this to me."

"That was because I asked him not to," replied Stanley. "He also said that he was aware of your gambling problem."

Shane appeared slightly shaken by this statement, but nevertheless he went on the attack. "What gambling problem? I haven't got a gambling problem."

It was Derek's turn to ask the next question. "Do you go to Cat-Haven dog track to gamble on greyhound racing, Shane?"

Shane swivelled round in his chair. He thought

for a few moments before answering. "I have been there occasionally."

Derek continued. "That's not what we heard. We heard that you go to every meeting, which we believe is twice a week. A bit more than occasionally, wouldn't you say?"

"Sir Lancelot doesn't spend much time in Cat-Haven in the winter. How would he know?"

"We didn't get that information from Sir Lancelot," said Stanley. "We got it from Honest Arnold, a bookmaker that you've lost a lot of money to. He told us you go to practically every meeting, and mostly lose a lot of money."

"Your face is as white as a vanilla ice cream, Shane, but not as lickable!" Derek grinned, enjoying his joke.

Shane said nothing.

"That would seem to give you a motive for stealing from Sir Lancelot's safe," said Stanley.

Again Shane said nothing.

"We know that you had a key to Willy Splish's office," said Stanley, changing the direction of the questioning. "And you used it to enter his office and plant five of the rubies you had stolen from Sir Lancelot."

"That's nonsense," replied Shane, beginning to get a little more colour back in his cheeks. "You have absolutely no proof. And that's because I've never been to Willy Splish's office."

At that moment there was a knock on the interview room door. It was swiftly opened to reveal Katie, who crossed the room and whispered something in Stanley's ear.

"This interview is suspended at ...." Stanley looked up at the clock on the wall. ".... at 11.31 a.m." He switched off the tape recorder and got up from the desk. He, Derek and Katie left the room.

The sound of the key turning in the lock shattered the silence that had descended on the interview room. Shane put his head in his hands for a few moments, his breathing harsh, a sweat breaking out on his forehead.

The Same Day

P amela was waiting in Stanley's office when Stanley, Derek and Katie came through the door. The first thing she did was to tell Stanley and Derek that it was Katie who had solved the mystery of the torn scrap of paper. She went on to tell them everything that had happened at the Cat-Haven Arsenal warehouse, mentioning the invoice addressed to William Sticker.

"Here's a copy of the invoice, Chief," said Pamela.

"And even better than that," said Katie, "look at this." She pulled a photograph out of a yellow folder. "Firearms Fergie from the Cat-Haven Arsenal took this on his mobile, and I've had it printed up. This is William Sticker."

Derek snatched it from Katie's paw. "You were right, Stan. The guilty cat *is* Ship-Shape Shane. This proves he bought the dynamite to blow up Sir Lancelot's safe. I've always suspected him."

"It's certainly a strong piece of evidence, Chief,"

said Stanley. "Well done Katie. That was a great piece of detective work."

Katie blushed. "Thanks, Sarge. I also thought it might be useful if Firearms Fergie could come in to the station to confirm that it was Shane he sold the dynamite to. He said he'd be happy to. Shall I give him a call now? He said he could come in straightaway if we needed him."

"Good idea, Katie. Yes, give him a call." Katie took out her Blackberry.

"Chief," said Stanley. "I suggest we let Shane stew for a while until Fergie comes in. Once he's here we can put Fergie in Interview Room 2, and then continue with Shane."

"What about the murder?" asked Pamela.

Stanley smiled. "I'm sure he did it, and I've got something up my sleeve."

The Same Day

Forty five minutes later Stanley and Derek returned to interview room one. Firearms Fergie was now sitting in interview room two, together with Jack and Marmaduke. Stanley re-started the tape machine and updated the time.

"Shane," said Stanley slowly, "we're going to return to the matter of the rubies a little later. There's something else we want to pursue with you at this time." Stanley paused, and pointedly looked over Shane's shoulder at Derek. Shane just managed to turn round in time to see Derek nodding his agreement. Stanley and Derek had planned to do this before entering the interview room, in order to unnerve Shane. The expression on Shane's face suggested that the tactic had worked. Stanley withdrew the copy invoice from Cat-Haven Arsenal and pushed it across the desk towards Shane. "Can you explain what this is, Shane?" Stanley was sure that a flash of fear registered in Shane's eyes.

"Never seen it before," said Shane, trying his best to stay calm, although inside he was a bundle of nerves.

"You're lying, Shane." Stanley leaned forward and reached under the desk. "I can tell you're lying – your mouth's moving!" With his right paw Stanley pushed the button that was concealed under the desk. The wooden panel along one wall slid back to reveal a two-way mirror. They were looking straight into the adjoining room, interview room two. Stanley kept his eyes fixed on Shane's face. He was clearly shocked to see Firearms Fergie in the next room talking to the two police cats who had brought him in to the cat-police station.

"I think you know the cat who is helping us with our enquiries," said Derek. Shane did not respond.

Once more Stanley pressed the button underneath the desk, and the wooden panel slid back into place. "Do you still deny knowledge of this invoice, Shane?"

"Of course."

Stanley now pulled out a copy of the photograph of Shane that Fergie had taken on his mobile. The background clearly showed that it had been taken in the Cat-Haven Arsenal warehouse. "You and William Sticker are one and the same cat, are you not?"

"So what if I am?" responded Shane. "There's no crime in that."

"Why were you buying dynamite, Shane?" asked Derek.

Shane was silent.

"I suggest to you, Shane," said Stanley, "that you

bought it to blow up Sir Lancelot's safe. And then you stole the cash and the rubies that were in the safe."

"You have no proof," said Shane.

"The Harbour Master-cat saw you do it, didn't he?" said Derek.

"Or he suspected you of doing it?" said Stanley. "He accused you, didn't he? And to keep him quiet you killed him."

"That is such nonsense," said Shane. But he didn't sound convincing, and there was a nervous twitch round his right eye. "You're guessing."

"It's more than a guess," said Derek.

"You made one serious mistake, Shane." Stanley smiled a thin smile. He took a sheet of paper out of the yellow folder. "I'd like to take you back to the morning of Bosun Brian's murder. You were interviewed by Cat-Constables Jumping Jack and Marmalade Marmaduke in the Brixcat Yacht Club office in the harbour. I'm reading from their interview notes. You claimed that you didn't know where the safe *was* on Sir Lancelot's yacht. Considering you were in charge of looking after Sir Lancelot's yacht that was pretty stupid of you. It immediately brought suspicion on you!"

"Is that all you've got? Is that what you're basing your claims on?" Shane laughed.

"You won't be laughing for long, Shane," said Derek.

"I only mentioned that," said Stanley, "to point out to you that you're not as clever as you think you are,

Shane." Stanley referred to the interview notes once more. "When Cat-Constable Jumping Jack asked you what you knew about the Harbour Master-cat's death, you replied, and these were your exact words ....." Stanley read from the printed sheet of paper, "'.... only that he fell in the sea and hit his head on something.'"

"So," said Shane rudely.

Stanley continued reading from the notes, "and when asked how you knew that he was dead, you replied 'Nosey Nathan told me."

"Well he did."

"Your mistake, Shane, was to say that Brian had hit his head on something. My cat-colleague, Chief Inspector Dimwit, was the cat who mentioned that Bosun Brian was dead in front of Nathan, and that was the only information that Nosey Nathan had at that time. Chief Inspector Dimwit did not mention anything about Bosun Brian's head. Shortly after that, when we left Nathan in his booth, we saw you approaching. We didn't know who you were then, but you're quite easy to recognise, what with your beard and the fact that you always seem to be wearing a captain's hat. No doubt that was when Nathan told you that Brian was dead. The only way you could possibly have known that the back of his head was injured, was because *you* had caused that injury, by hitting him on the back of the head with the boathook."

Shane looked devastated.

"It's time to confess, Shane," said Derek softly.

Two Days Later –
Wednesday 21st December

Two days later Shane's pawprint and DNA sample came back from Annie's laboratory. They were a positive match with what was found on the boathook, the painting and the Cat-Haven Arsenal invoice scrap of paper. In the presence of his solicitor Shane made a full confession. The twenty missing rubies were found tucked away in a corner of his loft. He told Stanley and Derek that he had spent about half of the cash he had stolen from Sir Lancelot's safe. He had given it to Honest Arnold, the bookmaker from the Cat-Haven Greyhound Track. Stanley suspected that Honest Arnold was unlikely to volunteer to return it to Sir Lancelot, even though it was stolen money. Derek had decided that it was not a matter for the Cat-Haven Cat-Police to follow up. A decision arrived at mostly, Stanley suspected, because Sir Lancelot had been so disrespectful to them. And Stanley certainly wasn't going to lose any sleep over it!

The end of case Celebration Dinner was, as usual, held in the Juicy Grape Wine Bar. Stanley had started this tradition as a way of cat-team bonding, and it was now a regular occurrence at the end of a big case. It was an evening of fun and good food. Every detective-cat in the Cat-Haven Cat-Police was there. As usual Cheerful Charlie and several of the uniform police-cats were left in charge of the Cat-Police station.

Stanley always wore a special outfit for the Celebration Dinner. Tonight he was wearing his newest pair of smart pants, which he had bought at TK Katz. They were white linen trousers with red and green swirls, and looked dazzling. Unusually he was not wearing a waistcoat or a bow tie, but simply a red shirt, with green collars and cuffs.

"Wow! You look awesome, Stan," said Annie when they had first arrived at the wine bar. Unfortunately she hadn't realised that Derek was standing right behind her. He had turned up in a pair of old jeans and a crumpled grey shirt. When she realised that he had heard every word that she had said to Stanley, she was embarrassed. "Oh .... you look ..... er ..... good too, Chief."

Jack, who had also heard Annie's remarks, whispered in Marmaduke's ear, "I think the Chief must have forgotten to do his ironing, Marmy!"

* * * *

Twenty one cats sat round the huge 'H' shaped table in the private function room, away from the prying eyes of the cat-public. This meant that they could be as wild as they liked! They were served a fabulous five course dinner. Even Tammy had nothing but praise for the quality of the food. Wine and beer flowed freely for the older cats. The younger ones had to be satisfied with Cat-Cola or Six-Up.

After dinner it was time for games, like Blind Cats Buff, Snakes and Kittens, and Pin the Tail on the Mackerel. And of course the famous bread throwing competition. This was played throughout the evening. Stanley had a bell to announce each round of the competition. Every time the bell sounded three cats had to stand up and throw a piece of bread at another cat. Points were awarded for a direct hit, but of course the cat under threat could weave and duck to try and avoid being hit. Extra points were awarded for any piece of bread that hit another cat flush on the nose or mouth. Stanley decided the scores and in the case of any dispute his decision was final. Stephen filled in the scorecard.

At the end of the evening the scores were totted up. The cat with the least number of points would have to eat the 'Magic Treat', a disgusting, dirty brown mess of mulch. It was a dish of bread and cream and custard, mixed together with ketchup and mustard. It was vile!

Stanley asked Stephen to read out the scores, starting with the cat who had most points, and ending with the cat who had the fewest. When Stephen read out the list and reached the last two, every cat knew that the 'Magic Treat' was destined for either Cynthia or Stephen.

Stephen stood up and announced that he had seven points, but Cynthia had six. Poor Cynthia was dippy, daffy, scatty, ratty, loony, loopy and potty! And downright dizzy as well! She just couldn't believe her bad luck.

"Can I have a look at the scorecard, Stephen?" said Stanley.

Stephen's face was a strong shade of red, as he handed over the scorecard.

"Do you think he cheated, Jackster?" whispered Marmaduke to his best mate.

Stanley clicked his pen and counted up the scores. "I think you've made a mistake, Stephen," he said. "I make it that Cynthia also scored seven points, making it a tie between her and you."

"Very naughty," said Jack, nudging Marmaduke in the ribs. "I wonder what Stan'll do?"

"Ordinarily," Stanley began, "I would assume that you simply made a mistake, Stephen. But since you keep telling us all that you're so clever, so much *more clever* than all of us, it's hard to think that you could possibly have made a simple mistake like that!"

There were hoots of laughter around the table.

"So I've decided to deduct one point from your score for .... well .... cheating, which ..... let me see now .... yes .... that means that you're the winner of the 'Magic Treat'!"

There was more laughter and applause, and even hoots of derision.

"Serves you right, you clever clogs!" shouted Marmaduke.

"You had that coming, know-it-all!" said Jack. "Ha! Ha! Ha!"

Stanley picked up the phone on the table. "Send in the bread pudding, please."

A few moments later a waitress-cat brought in a large bowl of the mulch, and Stanley signalled her to put it in front of Stephen.

"EAT .... EAT .... EAT!" came the cry from round the table.

Stephen slowly picked up the spoon. He closed his eyes and put a spoonful of the horrendous mixture into his mouth.

"EAT .... EAT .... EAT!"

After only three mouthfuls Stephen jumped up from his chair. "I'm going to be sick!" he wailed. With an expression of great regret on his face, Jack managed to trip Stephen up. "Sorry, Stephen, that was real bad luck!"

Marmaduke was quick to back up Jack. "Yes, it was reeally, reeeally, reeeeally unlucky, Stephen!"

In fact it was more than unlucky for Stephen. As he struggled to stand up again, he was unable to prevent himself from vomiting on the spot. He was violently sick, the ghastly yellow spew that came out of his mouth going all over his shirt and trousers.

"Yuck!" exclaimed Tammy and Pamela at the same moment.

"Oh, look, there are chopped up carrots in it!" laughed Jack.

"Yuck is about right!" said Katie, but with a huge grin on her face.

Without doubt the happiest cat in the room was Cynthia. She had been saved from a horrible fate!

When Stephen had cleaned himself up as best he could, and their favourite waitress-cat had done her best to clean the carpet, Stanley pinged his glass and stood up.

"Before I read you the end of case poem I've composed, I do have one announcement to make. We're all very happy that Katie has joined us, and I think we all know that she's made a fabulous start to her career in the Cat-Haven Cat-Police. In recognition of that, the Chief and I ...." Stanley paused to glance at Derek, who nodded his head and smiled. ".... have decided to promote her from cadet-cat to the rank of cat-constable. So now she will be known as Cat-Constable Kool Kat Katie!"

"Just love the alliteration, Stan!" shouted out Jack.

"Agreed, Jack," said Stanley. "In fact the alliteration is .... sooooo cool!"

There were smiles all around the table, and lots of applause.

Katie looked slightly embarrassed, but there was no doubt she was very happy.

"And now for the Harbour Mystery Poem," said Stanley. All the cats round the table fell silent, and gave Stanley their full attention.

"To Brixcat Harbour we came,
To find out who was to blame
For the theft of some rubies off of a yacht,
That was owned by a cat that did smile such a lot.
Then after that, much to our shock and dismay,
A death did we find 'ere the end of the day!
At first we did think it might've been Bert.
'Cos Brian he had threatened to hurt.
And Mackerel Mike was a suspect we thought,
When we discovered a plane ticket he'd bought.
Then we did look at the cat who does paint,
And soon did we find he was not a saint.
Next we checked out the cat who's called Shane,
Then before long it all became plain.
When we knew he had lied, so hard did we press,
That 'twas no wonder he just had to confess!
'Cos we gave it our soul, and we gave it our heart,
d for criminal-cats we're much much too smart!"

294

THE END

*Now read the first chapter of Alexander Martin's
next book in the Stanley Smartpants series,*

Stanley Smartpants and the Poisoned Parrots

*To be published in 2013, and available online at
www.stanleysmartpants.co.uk*

Chapter 1

Monday 15th July

S tanley Smartpants sat at his desk reading the sports pages of the Cat-Haven Chronicle. As a former England footballer himself, he had watched last night's match with great enthusiasm. Wayne Spooney had scored a fantastic goal for England to defeat Pawtugal one nil in the opening match of the Cat-Euro championships.

Suddenly his office door burst open, and Jumping Jack almost fell into the room. "Just had an amazing phone call, Sarge. You're not going to believe this!" Jack was gasping for breath.

Stanley closed his newspaper. "Calm down, Jack," he said slowly. "Tell me what's happened."

"We've had a call from Pretty Polly's Pet Shop. When Polly opened the shop this morning ...." Jack took a deep breath. ".... she discovered half a dozen of her parrot cages were wide open. Six of her parrots had disappeared. And here's the strange thing. All the missing parrots were green."

"What do you mean?"

"She's got loads of parrots, all different colours, but only the green ones had been stolen!"

"Very curious," said Stanley to himself. He picked up the phone on his desk, and pressed a couple of buttons. It was ages before he heard the click of someone picking up. "Morning, Chief. We've got some missing parrots. Seems like they've been stolen." All Stanley could hear at the other end of the phone was a strange chomping, munching noise.

There was a painfully long pause before Chief Inspector Derek Dimwit finally spoke. "Do I have to deal with it now, Stan?" he mumbled. "I'm in the middle of my eggy toast."

"Problem is, Chief, they've been stolen from Pretty Polly's Pet Shop."

Derek continued to munch on his toast. "So?"

"She's a friend of your cousin the mayor."

"Flip!" said Derek in annoyance. "I'd forgotten that. I suppose we'll have to go round there. Give me five minutes, Stan."

Ten minutes later, Stanley and Derek left the Cat-

Haven Cat-Police Station in one of the blue panda cars from the yard and set off for Polly's Pet Shop.

As they reached the level crossing in the centre of town they were forced to pull up sharply. Although the barriers were up no traffic was moving. On the side where the road led down to the sea front, a queue of traffic had formed. On the town side of the barrier there was a chaotic scene. There was a lorry lying on its side. According to the sign writing it belonged to Old Catdonalds Farm in Cattington. A number of the milk churns it had been carrying had spilled out onto the road, and the ground was covered in a river of milk. A kitten was lapping up as much milk as he could, much to the annoyance of his mother, who grabbed him by the scruff of the neck and dragged him out of the milk puddle.

A large crowd of cats had gathered round, and Stanley spotted a motor bike lying on its side. Some twenty metres further away, stretched out on his back, was a cat wearing black leather trousers and jacket, and a bright blue crash helmet. He was lying perilously close to the railway line.

Stanley and Derek got out of their car and approached the crowd.

"We're the Cat-Haven Cat-Police," shouted Derek. "Stand back, please. Make room, make room. Let us through!"

One cat, who was kneeling beside the motorcyclist-cat, turned towards the source of the shouting, and held up his paw. "It's all right, officer, I'm a doctor. I'm just checking over this young cat. He's unconscious, I'm afraid." He carried on loosening the strap of the injured cat's helmet, and gently removed it. "Call an ambulance, please. This cat needs to go to hospital in a hurry. I think he's got a broken leg, and a few broken ribs. He's in a bad way. It would help me if you could organise some space for me. Move the crowd back."

"Don't worry, doctor," said Stanley, "we'll take care of it." He was already on his mobile phone calling 666, the cat emergency telephone service. He moved a few paces away and gestured to Derek to start moving the crowd back. When he had organised an ambulance, Stanley rang the cat-police station.

As soon as he had finished his call he went back over to the doctor-cat. "The ambulance is on its way, doctor. I've also arranged for one of our patrol cars to act as an escort, so it should be here soon." Stanley turned to Derek. "Let's see if we can find a witness, Chief. If you'd like to do that I'll check on the lorry driver-cat."

"Good idea, Stan. Any of you cats see what happened?" shouted Derek at the top of his voice.

Most of the cats who were looking on shook their heads, but one cat stepped forward. He was quite old, and walked with the aid of a stick. "I saw it, sir," he said. "The lorry came round the corner too fast and when the driver saw the red traffic lights he braked

The lorry driver-cat was pacing around, and sure enough he was singing softly in a very screechy voice.

"Old CatDonald had a farm .... E I E I O
And on his farm he had a cow ..... E I E I O
With a moo moo here and a moo moo there,
Here a moo, there a moo, everywhere a moo moo.
And the cows do give some milk,
That's always fresh and smooth as silk.
Old CatDonald's milk is best .... E I E I O
With free delivery as you've guessed .... E I E I O"

"He definitely ought to go to the hospital as well!" chuckled Stanley. "I think he needs a thorough check over!"

"You don't think he's got mad cow disease, do you Stan?"

"Good one, Chief," laughed Stanley.

and then skidded. He had obviously lost control of the lorry, and it crashed into the traffic lights, and turned over. All those milk churns spilled onto the road. Only a few seconds later that young cat lying over there came round the corner on his motorbike. One of the milk churns was rolling towards him and he somehow managed to avoid it. But he couldn't avoid a second milk churn and crashed into it. He then somersaulted head over paws over the handlebars of his bike and finished up where he is now. Then you arrived."

"Was any other vehicle involved?" said Derek.

"No, sir."

"Thank you. A patrol car will be here shortly, and one of my officers will take a statement from you."

"Oh dear! I'll be late for the Cat-Bingo."

A train heading for Torcat rumbled past. Startled cats peered out of the train windows at the sight of the accident. Some of them looked disappointed that they wouldn't be able to see more of what was going on. A few moments later the barriers went up. But none of the traffic moved.

Derek strode over to Stanley. "How's the lorry-driver cat?" he asked.

"Shaken and incredibly confused. He can't stop singing!"

"Singing? echoed Derek. "What's he singing?"

"Come over and listen, Chief."

* * * *

V